STORY SINGER

Also by Sheila Rance:

Sun Catcher
Storm Chaser

STORY SINGER

SHEILA RANCE

Illustrated by Geoff Taylor

Orion
Children's Books

First published in Great Britain in 2014
by Orion Children's Books
an imprint of Hachette Children's Group
a division of Hodder and Stoughton Ltd

1 3 5 7 9 10 8 6 4 2

The paper and board used in this paperback are natural and
recyclable products made from wood grown in sustainable forests.
The manufacturing processes conform to the environmental
regulations of the country of origin.

A catalogue record for this book
is available from the British Library.

ISBN 978 1 4440 1525 6

Printed by Clays Ltd, St Ives plc

www.orionchildrensbooks.co.uk

For Theo and Robyn

Maia

'Maia felt the song enter her bones.
She needed to run, to leap, to fly, to be free.
It was singing her name. "Sun Catcher."'

Maia the flame-haired.
Maia the outsider.
Maia, the stolen princess.

Always an outsider, headstrong Maia longs for
life outside the watery world of the Cliff Dwellers.
Frightened of the sea, she dreams of training a hunting
eagle, but when she is named Sun Catcher she
discovers her destiny lies in a distant land.

Kodo

'Above him the silk hung waiting.
Kodo grasped a strip, tearing it from the thorns.
The silk was shrieking, commanding
him to free it . . .'

**Kodo the lizard boy,
dreamer, friend, thief.**
longs to leave the stilt village and his life
as an untouchable. His friendship with Maia
is forbidden. Valiant, loving and true of heart,
yet vulnerable to the silk's power, he will lie,
steal and betray to possess it.

Razek

'She called me Storm Chaser.
Storm winds destroy the weed beds.
You are the storm I chased, Flame Head.
I can't go back without you now.'

Razek the Storm Chaser,
the arrogant weed-master.
Driven by his love-hate relationship
with Maia, he first endangers her by
bringing the Wulf Kin to their village,
then deserts his people to protect her.

Tareth

*'A tall dark-haired figure swinging
on crutches, as if blown by storm-winds.
A man with eyes of fire and
an eagle feather in his hair.'*

Tareth, the Warrior Weaver

of the singing silk.
An Eagle Hunter driven by his promise to protect Maia.
Maia calls him father, but is he?
His life is not his to give.
Long ago, the mysterious singing silk claimed him.

Elin

*'A beautiful woman, with eyes like blue ice
and red hair that tumbled down her shoulders.
She held herself like a queen, but her robes
were worn, the fabric frayed.'*

Magnificent. Dangerous.
Death Bringer.

Elin is ruthless in her desire to destroy
her lost sister and claim the power of the sun-stone.
Imperious and corrupt, she believes she can catch
the power of the sun, only to find that some
things burn even brighter than her hatred.

Caspia

'Caspia glanced at her, grinned and took
hold of the sun-stone. Maia closed her eyes and
waited for the scream and the smell of burning.
Nothing happened. She heard the Wulf Kin
exhale beside her, as if he too
had feared for the girl.'

Caspia, the thought thief.
Raised as a pawn in her parents' pursuit of
power, spoiled, damaged Caspia is no puppet.
As duplicitous and ambitious as her mother,
she dreams that one day she will seize power,
and bend Khandar to her cruel, childish will.

Var

*'Var hesitated. He wasn't good with words.
He preferred silence. There had been
too much noise in the Sun City.
Things there he would rather forget.'*

Var the assassin.
Deadly, silent, secret, relentless.
Summoned to kill the Sun Catcher.
Loyal to his master, his knives and his black rat.
Var must choose between light and dark
and discover a hidden destiny.

Azbarak

'He knows where his loyalty lies.
The city is as good as ours once Azbarak
sees the Wulf Kin riding with me.
Azbarak does what is best for Azbarak.'

Azbarak the Keeper.

Guardian of the Sun City. A man of many faces,
jewels and embroidered coats, with a child army of
thieves ready to do his bidding. A servant of the old
regime, he will protect the city come what may.

PROLOGUE

I t was a good day to die.

Frost glinted in mossy gullies, an eagle soared on the updrafts, bronze leaves trembled on wind-stunted trees. Far below, the river thundered through the gorge, smashing stones and wood and wild water against rock falls. Rainbows arced over the torrent, catching spray that drifted like smoke. She was too late to cross. The ice had vanished with the sun-catch.

She could leap over the edge and it would be over. Dashed against rock, drowned in snow-melt. Her body beached on the gravel beds of the Unending River as it swept towards the Sun City. Her bow shattered. Her spirit in the wind. An ending.

She turned and searched for the hunters and their beasts. They were close. Too close. Beasts maddened by the smell of blood. Killers, frantic to leap and tear, to crush and snap her bones. She had failed. Her message would die with her.

She was afraid.

The large spotted cat panting at her feet staggered upright. She touched the tawny head. She could feel the growl vibrating through his skull into her hand.

'Travel swiftly, my old friend!' she whispered.

She would not go lightly into the dark of death. Not

without taking them with her.

Her hands shook as she fitted an arrow in her bow. The Wulf Kin would pay for this treachery. She must kill again and drag one more of their bestial spirits with her. She heard a howl as her arrow struck. The hunters stooped to release their wulfen.

She should have hidden when she heard the baying in the valley. Should have sent the spotted cat on alone with the silk braid from her bow. A warning. But the Wulf Kin had moved too fast. She had been too tired, too hurt, too slow. Altara would perish. So would she.

She raised her arms. The sun flared in the silver tips of her bow. The silk braid unravelled. The wind sang. A single voice – clear and cold, distant as the spinning stars – chimed, commanding her. Her silk was singing. The river would carry her towards the Sun City.

It was a good day to die.

CHAPTER ONE

Maia woke suddenly. Beside her Nefrar twitched. His long spotted tail lashed against her boots. She felt the big cat's claws stretch and retract, raking the earth. A growl rumbled in his chest.

It looked like the cheetah was in the grip of a night-wake. She wondered if the old silk hidden in her back-sack had whispered and disturbed him. Silk dreams had kept her awake despite being tired to the bone after escaping from the Marsh Lord. She touched the bag. The silk was safe.

The hunting cat stirred. She put her hand on his neck. His fur was raised. It was rough to touch. His skin shivered beneath her fingers, rippling like the wind blown shallows of the sun-deeps.

'What is it? Have they found us?'

Nefrar rolled to his feet and stood, staring into the darkness.

Maia reached for her knife, slipping it from its sheath. She could see two long bundles stretched on the ground. The Watcher, who had promised that she and her crows would guide them across the Vast. And Var, who'd sworn to protect her. Both were asleep. Another shadow crouched close by keeping watch.

'Kodo?'

'Did I wake you?' The lizard boy's voice was muffled. He swallowed and yawned.

'Something's happening,' said Maia.

Kodo got to his feet. Maia heard a faint clink as he reached for his fishing spear. Felt his warmth as he stood beside her, staring into the darkness.

'Nefrar woke me. He can hear something.'

'Has the Marsh Lord found us?'

They listened. The quiet of sun-sleep flowed around them. Tiny pinpricks of light gleamed through the web of branches above her head. She could see the pale tip of the horned moon. Her eyes searched the dark. Nothing.

'Nothing!' Kodo echoed her thought.

Maia held her breath, straining to probe beyond the hollow. She heard the slow, soft breaths of her companions. The rustle of feathers as the Watcher's red-legged crows roosted in the trees. They hadn't been followed.

Nefrar lowered himself to the ground.

'Whatever alarmed him has gone,' said Maia.

She slid her knife into its sheath and lay down beside the big cat, resting her head on her back-sack. She could hear his steady breathing. He was calm. There was nothing to fear.

Nefrar's snores deepened. He sounded like Azbarak, the

4

fat Keeper. She thought about how Azbarak had taken her to the gates of the Sun City so that she and her companions could make their way to the cliff village and the moth-garden. She must return swiftly. They would leave when it was light. She fell asleep, remembering the sound of the city gates closing behind her.

CHAPTER TWO

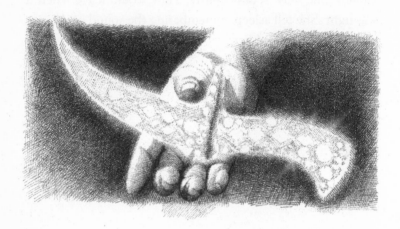

I t was hot.
Azbarak the Keeper mopped his sweating forehead. The heat bounced off the sand. The oasis shimmered beyond the dunes, a mirage in the bright sunlight. He urged his horse forward. It slid down the sand, found firmer footing and plodded towards the distant village stronghold.

He wondered if leaving the Sun City had been wise. But there had been no news. Var had vanished. So had the flame-headed Sun Catcher and her friends. And Elin, the defeated Queen, had escaped into the mountains.

Too many unknowns. Too much uncertainty.

He needed runners and seekers to search for the fleeing Queen, he needed to discover her plans while he watched over the sun-stone in the Sun City.

He kicked his horse on, anxious to reach the sprawling

holdfast at the edge of the hills. He must know if the Sun Catcher would return with the silk. He hoped that Var had sent a message.

The boy would not fail him. He had found him wandering alone in the desert. Var owed him his life.

A group of children sat on the high wall. A bright green bird with a long, sweeping tail perched beside them. It screeched an alarm and flew down into the garden as Azbarak trotted past. The children scrambled after it, rushing to the gate, swinging it open and standing aside as he rode into the courtyard.

As he swung from his horse, groaning with the effort, they mobbed him. Swarming over his horse, like a pack of bright-eyed tree rats, they tugged the gaudy bundles from his saddle, pulling them open, spilling the contents across the grass. They patted his clothes, stealing from his pockets, chattering like the pied birds feasting on the apricots in his trees.

'Enough!' he bellowed, grabbing the small boy who was slipping the curved knife from his belt. The jewels in the hilt blazed in the sunlight as he held the child aloft and shook him. 'Is this how I taught you to greet me?' He glared at the children. 'Thieves, all of you.'

The children scattered, clutching the booty they had taken from the bundles.

'They are pleased to see you, Keeper.' A tall, thin girl, her dark hair in a plait which reached below her waist, caught the horse's bridle. 'And the gifts you always bring.'

'And you, Nimah. What gift do you expect me to bring?'

She flipped her plait over her shoulder as she led the horse towards a building set at the edge of the garden, her strides sure and graceful. The silver discs on her anklet chimed as she moved.

'Stories, Keeper. Always stories.'

She waited for Azbarak to reach her. 'And to hear why you have come. Are you returning to the Sun City?'

Azbarak wiped the beads of sweat rolling down his cheeks. 'I can't stay long. I will need runners. There are messages to send. Secrets to hear.'

Nimah nodded. 'They are ready. Though none are as swift as Var.'

'Has he returned?'

She shook her head. 'Do you expect him?'

'He serves another.'

'The new Queen?'

'Perhaps.'

Nimah smiled. 'And this makes you angry.'

'He is beyond my reach,' grumbled Azbarak. 'The old ways are changing.'

'We heard rumours. Felt the wind change. Grow warm. Heard stories of snow-melt and the thunder of new rivers.'

'The sun was caught,' said Azbarak.

He wiped the sleeve of his embroidered coat across his forehead. And realised that his gold thumb ring, with its chunk of amber, bright as an eagle's golden eye, was missing. He hadn't felt the theft.

Nimah laughed. She held up her hand. The jewel shone. She tossed it to him. 'I will keep it the next time I take it.'

Azbarak slipped the ring on his thumb. 'Has Var sent word?' he called after her.

'He will return. He always does. Where else would he go? You are the Keeper.'

Azbarak mounted the steps into the cool shade of the house. The floor was littered with scraps of cloth. On each lay the trinkets he had wrapped in bundles and hung on the saddle or hidden beneath his coat. He smiled as he counted them. The thieves had done well.

The smell of his favourite supper greeted him. The still calm of the house fell about his shoulders. The heat and discomfort of the journey was forgotten. Nimah was right. Var always came back. He had nowhere else to go.

CHAPTER THREE

Maia wriggled towards the top of the ridge and peered down. Below was their final descent. Beyond stretched the Vast, an endless green plain vanishing into the purple distance. Somewhere far from sight lay Altara, the Warrior Women's stronghold. She would take the moon-moths' cocoons and eggs, and the strips of old silk, across the plains to the safety of the holdfast. Once there she must travel swiftly to Tareth in the Sun City. He needed the silk.

Kodo squeezed in beside her, breathless from the last scramble. He pulled out his knife to slash back the tangle of brambles that snagged his tunic. The silk hidden in the sheath sighed.

'No wonder they say it's impossible to cross,' he said quickly, hoping that Maia hadn't heard the faint whisper.

She hadn't. She was remembering when she had first seen

the never-ending grasslands. She had gone into the Vast with Xania, the Story Singer, running till her feet were raw, fear snapping at her heels, afraid that the Wulf Kin would catch them. She remembered the Singer dying from the Wulf Kin blade. Remembered the snow covered burial mound on the edge of the Cloud Plains. She touched her lips with her fingertips.

'Xania. Story Singer. Go well, sister.'

She flicked her fingers sending her thoughts into the Vast. With her sister dead, there was no Story Singer to tell the tales of Khandar. Maia blinked away the sudden burn of tears. When the silk was safe she must find a new Singer to wear the story-coat.

'So that's the Vast. It's like the far-deeps,' said Kodo, his voice husky. 'It has no end. It rolls and moves like waves.'

'Until it reaches the mountains,' said Maia.

'And the Sun City.' Kodo licked the scratches on his hands. 'I'll be glad to be away from here.'

Maia beckoned to the Watcher.

'The plains are empty,' she called. 'We are alone.'

The Marsh Lord and his hounds had not crossed this far. The Wulf Kin were not hunting across the grasslands. Only long shadows chased across the grass as tall clouds massed above the hill. They hid the sun. She shivered.

The Watcher joined her.

'We'll go down.'

The old woman glanced at the thunderclouds. 'I will mark your path when we see the stars.'

Maia nodded. She must run under stars and sun. She had to return to the Sun City quickly.

Before the cold of wolf-walk brought the snows she must help Tareth make a new moth-garden. He would tease silk from the cocoons she carried in her back-sack. Set others aside so that the grubs could emerge. By the next sun-catch, moon-moths would fly among the thorn bushes in the silk garden. Her father would grow strong and weave and fly KiKya, the eagle she had stolen from its nest.

She would never fly eagles. That dream was lost. She was the Sun Catcher. Her fire had harmed KiKya. She couldn't hunt with eagles, but she could find a new Story Singer to carry Xania's stories across Khandar.

Kodo watched Var push through the trees, picking up speed as the slope grew steeper. He lost his footing and tumbled through the undergrowth, his progress marked by the sound of breaking branches and the clatter of stones.

'Won't be anything to hunt,' Kodo muttered. 'His noise will scare everything away.'

Maia tightened the straps of her back-sack as a gust of wind tugged at her. She gasped as the skies split open. Sudden rain hammered against her like spears flung from the hands of a screaming army. The Vast disappeared. The wind howled, tearing shallow-rooted trees from the ground.

'We must shelter,' she shrieked.

The Watcher's reply was torn to shreds. Maia reached to help her. The wind knocked her off her feet. The earth seemed to shudder.

The Watcher staggered, her robes filled like the sails of Trader's boat. Grabbing her as she passed, Kodo was slammed against a tree. Desperately he clung to a branch. Stinging ice stones battered his face. A deluge of rain soaked him.

Maia struggled to her knees.

The sky was dark. The wind roared. One of the Watcher's crows was blown over the ridge.

The Watcher hauled herself up and hung on to Kodo as the wind tried to tear them from the tree. He and the Watcher flung themselves to the ground as the sapling was uprooted.

'The Storm Chaser,' howled Kodo. 'He's trying to stop you leaving!'

Kodo had never liked Razek. He had helped save the Weed Master from drowning but he wouldn't ever call him a friend. The Lizard People didn't trust the Cliff Dwellers.

'The Catcher saved his life. Why would the Storm Chaser try to harm her?' demanded the Watcher. She sat up, water pouring from her sleeves and down her hooked nose.

'Because!' shouted Kodo. 'Because he would! Because he can! Look at the storm clouds. He's called them.'

Maia shook her head. 'Razek wouldn't summon a storm. He can't.'

'He can chase storms . . . send one where he wants it to go.'

'No!' cried Maia. 'Razek wouldn't.'

'He may be trying to delay Helmak, the Marsh Lord.' The Watcher pulled her soaking hood over her hair. 'When he discovers that you have escaped, Catcher, Helmek will follow to see where the Trader makes a landfall. And if he finds him and discovers that Laya's story is untrue then he will send his hounds to track us.'

Maia stared at the Watcher. 'Why will Laya say that we left with Trader?'

The old crone bared her yellow teeth. 'I told her it was

what she saw. She will tell Razek and the Marsh Lord.'

Maia wondered if the Salt Holder's daughter would have the courage to lie to the Marsh Lord. Laya would be glad that her rival was leaving.

'Then let's hope her story is believed,' she rubbed the fur of the cheetah crouched at her side. 'Laya is a poor liar.'

As if in reply, the wind tossed the faint sound of a horn above their heads.

'The Marsh Lord,' gasped Kodo.

The Watcher called. 'Come. The storm will hide us and drown our scent.'

And put out the fire Maia had started in the moth-garden, thought Kodo.

A snaking shaft of lightning shot from the sky, blasting the stunted tree beside her. It caught light.

Kodo scrambled to his feet, his face and hair blue in the eerie glow.

'Come on. It'll kill us all!'

He grabbed Maia.

The Watcher lifted her arms and faced the storm. Lightning forked towards them, striking the ground, splitting rocks. Flickering light encircled them, tongues of fire spitting and hissing as the rain touched them.

She stepped across the dark ring of singed grass, tugging a bundle of feathers from her sleeve.

She raised her hand. Maia recognised the feathered bag that held the Watcher's coloured stones. The runes. She could see the Watcher shaking them at the storm clouds, shouting at the sky. She saw a crow fall from her sleeve and watched it tumble away.

14

The Watcher stumbled after it.

'This isn't the Storm Catcher's doing. Come,' she called again. 'Quickly.'

Maia and Kodo plunged over the edge after her.

They cowered, gasping in the tall grass. Kodo pressed his fist into his side to ease the pain. Maia thought her heart would burst from her chest. The Watcher had collapsed. Var lay his hand on Nefrar's back. The cheetah gazed back the way they had come. Maia strained to hear the sounds of baying hounds, the call of a horn beneath the distant rumble of thunder.

'There's nowhere to hide here,' she panted. 'If the hounds and horses find a way down, the Marsh Lord will outrun us.'

'You go on. I will lay a false trail,' said Var.

'And I,' croaked the Watcher. 'Two scents will confuse the hounds.'

'And mine,' said Kodo as he swayed to his knees.

'No,' said Maia. 'We stay together. Fight together. We have Nefrar. We're strong. And the Marsh Lord will not dare to follow us into the Vast. He has no one to guide him.'

'Just our tracks. The way is no longer safe,' said the Watcher.

'The birds can guide us. And you can show us how to read the stars so that we can use the darkness.'

The Watcher shook her head. 'I have failed you, Catcher.

I should have sent you across the sun-deeps with Trader. I should have remembered what the stones know. I cannot guide you across the grasslands.'

She stared at the dark clouds. Then she turned her back, ignoring the spectacular light dance in the sky.

'The storm speaks. I cannot come across the Vast.'

'Cannot?' echoed Maia.

'Nor can I seek a way past the sands if you are to reach the Sun City safely. My crows would die in that arid land.'

'We're not going into the Hidden,' said Maia.

'I will guide you to the city. You need have no fear,' Var said.

'Who are you to tell us what we need? Who made you our guide?' snapped Kodo.

Var looked at him. 'I am Var. And I know the way past the Hidden to the city. I will take you to safety.'

Kodo bit back a retort. 'We should find Trader. He'll take us to Haddra. He'll look for a landfall in this storm. We will find him sheltering on the edge of the deeps.'

Maia wasn't listening. She was staring at the Watcher.

'The storm speaks?' she asked.

'The storm will not let me pass.' The Watcher glanced at the sky. 'You and your friends must leave. I can set you on the way. Show you the star path to follow. I must remain.'

'But we need you to guide us.'

'The boy and his rat will show you the path. He is your guide.'

'But . . .'

'I am the Watcher. I am needed here. I must watch those who stay. You must take the silk to the weaver. You will be faster without an old woman to slow you.' She peered at Var. 'I will teach you the star patterns. And how to use the wind and sun shadows.'

'I can follow the wind. I can remember star paths. I've sailed with Trader. He taught me. Show me the stars and I'll lead Maia across the Vast.' Kodo glared at Var, who was using his knife to strip the bark from a short stick. 'Why should Maia trust him to guide us? What do we know about him?'

Var looked up, his eyes mocking. He stuck his knife in the ground and held the peeled curls of bark for Tiki his rat to nibble.

This fuelled Kodo's rage. 'Where did he come from? He's not a Cliff Dweller, a Lizard Keeper, a Marsh Lord. He has no herds. No goods to trade. He keeps a rat!'

Var ignored him.

Kodo lunged and plucked the black knife from the ground. Tiki bit him. Kodo swore and shook the rat off his hand. He held up the knife.

'Is this carried by a guide?'

Var's rat grabbed the flatbread lying by Maia's back-sack and scurried into the shadows. 'Even his rat's a thief!' Kodo drew back his hand to hurl the knife.

'Kodo!' Maia seized his arm.

Kodo wrenched himself free. From the corner of his eyes he saw the tip of the rat's tail twitch and vanish, felt Var rise into a crouch, saw his fist clench and remembered.

'It was you!' he yelled as he launched himself at Var. 'This was the knife. You tried to kill Maia!'

Hauling ropes and reefing sails on the trader boat had

made him strong. He knocked Var flat as the boy pulled a knife from nowhere and clamped it to the earth. He swung his leg across Var, pinning him down.

'The knife in the market place. The black knife. It was yours. It's the same. There was a rat there too.'

Maia took the knife from Kodo's hand and twitched the second blade from Var's fingers. Both were black. Both had a design scratched into the handle. They were perfectly balanced throwing knives and she had seen one like them before.

'And the rat – *your* rat – bit Zena!' Kodo accused.

He grabbed Var's shoulders. 'You tried to kill Maia in the Sun City. It was your knife.'

Var wriggled and suddenly heaved. Kodo was tipped off balance and Var rolled away. He pulled a third knife from behind his shoulder and held it in front of him.

'If I had wanted to kill her she would be dead!' His dark eyes didn't leave Maia. He stuck the knife into the earth at his feet. Before Kodo could charge at him, he slipped another blade from his boot.

'And I'd have slit your throat with this, lizard boy!' The blade quivered next to the first as he flicked it into the ground.

'And me? Would I be dead too?' The Watcher hadn't moved.

Var shrugged. 'If I wished it.'

The Watcher smiled. 'And do you wish it?'

'No.'

Var slowly straightened, the tension draining from his shoulders. Even so, noticed Maia, he was poised, ready to spring. He was watching Kodo from the corner of his eye.

18

Ready to attack.

She flicked her wrists and the knives she held thudded into the ground next to Var's. She saw the surprise in his eyes. She had been well taught by Tareth and the Warrior Women.

'You carry many weapons for a guide,' she said.

'I . . . protect,' he said. 'There are many dangers.'

'What dangers?'

Var hesitated. He wasn't good with words. He preferred silence. There had been too much noise in the Sun City. Things there he would rather forget. He wondered how much of the truth she needed to hear. He wasn't her enemy. He would keep her safe as Azbarak had commanded. The Keeper didn't want her dead.

Tiki scurried from the shadows. Var scooped him up and stroked behind his ears. The rat sat in his palm, whiskers twitching. He heard Kodo's intake of breath and tucked Tiki inside his tunic.

'I will keep you safe too, brother,' he muttered. He felt the rat snuggle against his belt.

He looked at Maia. She stood like a spear, slim and straight. The rat didn't disgust her as it did the lizard boy. His knives hadn't frightened her. He would tell only what she might need to know. He wouldn't speak about Elin's summons or her daughter Caspia and her quest for silk. He wondered if Maia's back-sack held silk. She never let it leave her sight. But she would not always be so careful. If she carried any silk Tiki would find it. Azbarak would need to know.

'The Keeper knew. Azbarak sent me,' he said. 'He thought you would need protection.'

'He's lying,' said Kodo.

'Perhaps,' agreed Maia slowly. 'But he tried to rescue me. The Watcher sent him to find me.' She turned to the Watcher who sat, her bird bright eyes watching Var. 'Is what he claims true?'

The Watcher pulled out her feathered bag.

'The stones will know. Put your hand into the bag, carrier of many knives. The stones will tell us.'

Var suppressed a shudder as she held it out. It was a bird's skin. A dead crow. He could see a red jewel where the eye should be. Red legs and claws hung over the Watcher's bony fingers. She shook the bag. It rattled and chuckled. The Watcher bared her yellow teeth.

'Are you afraid, boy?'

Var's hands curled into fists. He wasn't a boy. Nor was he afraid of an old crone and her skin and stones. He stepped forward and plunged his fist into the bag.

His hand was sucked down into the endless darkness. He cried out. And felt the rest of his body drawn into the stifling, feathered dark.

CHAPTER FOUR

He was falling through heat and darkness. He could hear water below. He had tumbled into a sinkhole. His hands scrabbled against collapsing sand and sharp rock. He choked as he opened his mouth to yell and swallowed sand. He panicked. He would plunge into the watercourse cut into the rocks in the belly of the sand hills and drown.

But water didn't roar as it flowed slowly beneath the sand. He had seen it trickle in the rock channel in the garden at the edge of the Hidden. Had heard the green bird call as it had spread a tail painted with eyes and lowered its shining head to drink. Watched the jewels on Azbarak's fingers flash as he tossed seeds to the bird.

The roar must be the wind as it blew the towering, suffocating walls of sand across the Hidden. It buried him as it passed. Left him coughing, flailing arms and legs under the weight. He tried to curl away from the sharp stabbing spears that pierced his flesh.

He tumbled into a hunter's pit. He was skewered on spikes. Lying on the broken sticks that had hidden the pit. He remembered the terror. The loneliness. He could see the sun through the hole he had made as he fell. The light burned his eyes. Scorched his face. Blistered his lips. His tongue swelled. Turned black. Choked him. Silenced him.

The scream wasn't his. Snapping teeth and clawing talons ripped open his chest. The spotted cat tore at his flesh. Crunched his bones. Crushed his skull. He must call out. Beg the hunters to release him.

But the beast had eaten his tongue. He couldn't speak.

He held up his hands and grasped cool stones. Felt the chill of night. Heard the silence. Opened his eyes. And pulled his hand from the feathered bag as the night-wake dissolved.

Var stood, his head drooping, his fists clenched, aware of their eyes watching him. He shuddered.

'Well?' asked Kodo. His eyes were wide with shock as he looked from Var to the feathered bag and back again.

The Watcher flipped back her long sleeves, and cast the stones from the bag to the ground. She stirred them with her fingernail and looked up at Var. He made himself stand still beneath the searching gaze. Forced himself to meet her dark inquisitive stare. She had eyes like black beads. Like his rat, he thought.

'Well?' he echoed.

'Open your hand, boy. The stones have decided.'

Var's fists were clenched so tight he felt the bones grind. He drew a deep breath and opened his right hand. A white stone lay on his palm.

The Watcher nodded. 'What he told you is true,' she said slowly.

'Good,' said Maia.

Kodo said nothing.

Var knelt to retrieve his knives. His limbs were like water.

The Watcher gave him the feather bag. It was all he could do not to hurl it away. 'Return the stones,' she said. She swept the scatter of coloured stones towards him. 'Put them in the bag.'

Var thought about refusing. He never wanted to see or touch the bag of rocks again. It held night-wakes and horror. And fear. He knew he had been too weak to withstand its searching. He glanced at the Watcher. She said he had told the truth. Had the stones told her more? Trying to close his ears to their murmurs, he flipped them into the bag. He heard the cry of birds, the sigh of the sea, the crackle of a fire burning dry sticks, the hiss of hot winds blowing sand, the rattle of bones. He tossed the muttering bag to her.

She caught it, tucked it in her sleeve and rose to her feet.

'Come. I will show you the star trail.'

As Var followed her he heard Kodo whisper, 'Surely you don't believe it? I know he's lying.'

Maia's reply was too soft for him to hear.

The Watcher strode away from the camp. Once out of earshot she waited until Var reached her. She grasped his wrist, pulling him close. He could smell age and spices and dusty feathers.

'The stones know you, stranger. They found the truth. You will guide the Catcher.'

'Yes.'

'But they keep your secrets too. You chose the white stone. But there is another that chose you. It lies in your heart hand.'

Var stared at her. He had flicked them all into the bag. Had wanted nothing to do with them. He would never keep one of the talking stones. Yet the arm she held felt as hollow as the dark sinkhole. Slowly he opened his hand. He was holding a black stone.

'The keeper of secrets. The stone of darkness. Both the white and the black claim you. You must decide which to follow.' She dropped the white stone into his palm. 'You will always have to choose between the dark and the light.'

Var felt a shiver of disquiet. He tried to give her the stone. She pushed his hand aside.

'The stones are yours. Your truth. Your choice.'

'Choice?'

Var wondered if he had ever had a choice. He had always answered to others. To Azbrak's commands, to the summons of Elin, the red witch. He had even listened to the words of the red witch's daughter, seen her hunger for silk and watched her blood drip from his knife to seal their bond.

She watched him in silence. Finally she answered. 'The stones don't always make their understanding clear, even to me. You too have kept many things hidden from me. But the stones don't speak against you.'

Var dropped the pebbles inside his tunic. He felt Tiki squirm as the stones hit him. He had forgotten the rat was snoozing against his belt. He would hurl the runes away when he was alone on the Vast. He didn't want to be burdened by them. He wondered if the old woman thought she would be able to use them to tell her his thoughts for as long as he carried them.

He thought she had heard his plotting but she shrugged. 'So I must accept what they show. Since it seems that I cannot cross the Vast with the Catcher then you must go in my place. And I must be content that the stones have not tricked me.'

He felt the heat of her gaze. 'But, be warned. No harm can come to her. She must return the silk to the Weaver and find a Story Singer. She is the Sun Catcher and will defeat those who would try to steal her power. Many watch over her. She is not alone. The cat guards her. The lizard boy will defend her. The Storm Chaser will search the skies for signs that all is well. And I will send my birds. The Catcher will have no cause to fear.'

'The Catcher doesn't fear me.'

Unexpectedly the Watcher laughed. 'But you would do well to fear her. They call her Flame Head with good reason. Guide her well and you will be safe.'

Var decided not to allow the old woman to goad him into speech. He looked at the stars, searching for familiar points of light. Those he knew were low on the horizon.

The Watcher pointed to a different pattern, a cluster that outlined the shape of a running hound with the brightest light marking the tip of its nose.

'You will need to find that star. It will be the first to rise at sun-sleep and it stays low in the sky. You must walk towards the star hound. And travel as if the wind blows across the flight of your arrow. The sister stars must stay on your heart side. At sun-wake the sun will mark the path. Your shadow should be behind you if you have not lost your way.

The Watcher hesitated. 'It will be good to learn that the Catcher has reached the Sun City. She will be needed. Send word.'

She beckoned to Maia. 'You should leave. Go as far as you can before sun-wake. Sun-sleep is your friend.' She grasped Maia's hand. 'The stones have given the boy choices,' she murmured. 'I cannot tell what he will choose. But the cat Nefrar trusts him and the runes don't speak against him. I'll watch for signs.'

As they left her, the flashes of blue lightning still flickering in the clouds above her, she raised her fist, her silver bangles chiming and glinting.

'The sun's greeting, the wind's blessing, the earth's song be yours, Sun Catcher,' she called. 'And yours, Kodo, silk guardian.'

Kodo looked over his shoulder and almost tripped over his feet. He checked that his knife was secure and felt the tip scrape the tattered silk he had hidden there. He held his breath. The silk was silent. He stifled his disappointment. He had hoped the silk would whisper that he was right to mistrust Var. That he must keep Maia safe from the black throwing knives he carried. And he would make sure that the stranger didn't discover the bundles of silk and cocoons. The silk was Maia's secret. And his. He would keep it safe. He pushed his knife deeper into its sheath and saw an image of small lizards with a red-headed girl who looked like Maia.

It was Caspia, the girl who loved lizards and wanted silk too.

Chapter Five

The sky was blue, the sun bright. But the mountain air was cold. Caspia was glad of the fur over-tunic her father, Urteth, had given her. She pulled the hood of her cloak over her braided hair. He should hunt for a wolf to make her a hat like the Eagle Hunters wore. She couldn't ride and fly a fighting eagle in a hooded cloak. The flapping cloth would upset the half-wild eagles Urteth had captured.

She blew on her fingers to thaw them and picked a lump of bloody meat from the bowl at her feet. She tossed it high above the tower. Two eagles fell on it, talons extended. They tumbled, locked together, each fighting to snatch the flesh from the other. The chained eagle beside her screeched and launched himself from his post, desperate to fly and fight too. Caspia selected a smaller hunk of meat. It stuck to her fingers, the tiny ice crystals pricking them like needles.

The blood in the base of the bowl was already turning to icy mush. She peeled the deer meat away from her fingers, trying not to see the swollen white bodies of frozen maggots buried in the strings of venison. She hoped the cooks had fresher meat for the feast her mother had ordered for when the fires were lit and blazing in the sun hall.

She took a step away from the chained eagle and flicked the gobbet of food towards him. He fell on it but was ambushed by the winner of the sky battle. Unhampered by the trailing chain, the eagle dropped his prize to savage his foe, curving talons and stabbing beak ripping feathers from the scavenger's breast. It grabbed the meat and flew to perch on the battlements. The chained bird launched himself after it, was jerked tight on the end of its leash and fell back, screaming with rage.

Caspia selected another piece of rotting flesh.

'You'll make it weak. Teach it to lose a fight.'

She hadn't smelled the fur and leather and sweat scent of Vultek. The Wulf Kin stood close behind her. Caspia tossed the meat to the eagle before she turned to face him. He carried a hooded bird on his arm.

'I know what must be done. None of the eagles will fail,' she told him coldly.

Vultek tugged the hood from his eagle and cast it from his wrist. It was a clumsy gesture. Like most of his kind, he did not love eagles as her father and the Eagle Hunters did. She watched Vultek throw a piece of meat to his flying bird. It ignored it to soar on the updrafts.

The Wulf Kin took a larger piece of flesh.

'He will learn,' he said and stuffed the meat in his own

mouth, chomping it between his pointed teeth, lips open so she could see the bloody strands. Caspia swallowed her disgust. Vultek was useful. He was ambitious. He would follow her, do as she said.

'Then let's hope he will learn quickly.'

Vultek's gaze was sharp. 'Do you ride soon?'

Caspia shrugged. 'It's good to be prepared.'

Vultek turned to watch the eagles. 'It'll be many sun-wakes before the Wulf Kin have mastered them. Is Urteth wise to ask it of us? The wulfen are our weapons. Eagles and wulfen are poor companions in this cold place.'

'The fires in my father's halls are warm,' she replied, ice in her voice. 'And it's unwise to question his judgement.'

'Who questions Urteth's judgement?' Zartev had joined them.

Caspia felt the chill tentacles of dislike that flowed between the two Wulf Kin. Vultek wanted to oust the old soldier from his position as Urteth's trusted favourite. He thought she would support him against her father's champion. Zartev was old, his power dwindling, but his beast could still defeat any of the younger wulfen who challenged him. Vultek would have to kill him if he wanted to replace him and lead the Wulf Kin.

Caspia wondered if she could use their mutual dislike. She caught the old Wulf Kin's thoughts. He supported her. His loyalty was greater than Vultek's. She mustn't alienate him. But nor must she upset the ambitious upstart. He would be her security in the to-come. A queen needed her own band of Wulf Kin to form her guard.

She smiled at Zartev. 'No one. Vultek was saying that he

preferred to fight with wulfen. His eagle is still wayward.'

The old Wulf Kin grunted. 'Starve it. It will soon understand who is master.'

Vultek bit at the fleas crawling in the fur on the back of his knife hand. Caspia felt the tension between the two ebb away.

'Did you want me?' she asked the old Wulf Kin.

'Your mother has summoned you. She waits in the spear loft.'

Elin watched Urteth as he tested the balance of a throwing spear and examined the pine resin and bindings that fixed the flint spearhead to the slender shaft. Her fingers played with a pile of small bones, arranging them in stacks and lines. A flint-knapper was hammering rocks, breaking slivers of flint from the mother-stone. He took a leaf-shaped shard and started chipping flakes from the sides, making a sharp cutting edge.

As Caspia entered, Urteth nodded to the stone-shaper who put down his tools and silently left, taking a wide berth around the tall Wulf Kin. Zartev growled at him, the threat rumbling in his throat as the man scuttled past like a beetle. The Wulf Kin pushed the door shut and leaned on it, his long, furred arms folded across his bronze breastplate. Caspia hid her smile. If Vultek followed her to discover what was planned he would find the way barred.

'Where have you been, daughter?' demanded Elin.

'Watching the eagles.'

'Did they fly well?' asked Urteth.

'Most fought each other for the scraps the Wulf Kin tossed them,' said Caspia.

Urteth returned the spear he was holding to the stack of weapons propped against the wall. There were enough of the throwing and the shorter stabbing spears for an army, thought Caspia. Her heart raced.

'And the chained eagle fought too,' she said.

'Attacked the Wulf Kin?'

'No. Another eagle.'

'Good. We make progress.'

'But too slowly,' snapped Elin.

'The eagle will be tamed. It will lead the others. The Wulf Kin are not used to fighting with eagles. They must train their beasts to run with the birds. And train themselves too.'

'It is madness to think that the eagles will accept a leader.'

'They will accept me. And I will bind the chained eagle to my will. As I will the Eagle Hunters.' Urteth stroked the bronze guard which covered his wrist. 'They will not stand against us. Wulf Kin harry them. Few of their passes are safe. They are retreating high into the mountains. We will trap them there and hunt them down unless they join us.'

'We should strike now. Attack Altara as we planned. Burn it to the ground,' insisted Elin. 'Yanna and the Warrior Women will regret following the usurper.'

Urteth nodded. 'The Warriors already feel your anger. The wulfen roam free. The grasslands are no longer safe. The archers have withdrawn into their stronghold. They cannot hunt freely across the plains. The Wulf Kin are attacking their holdfast, just as you wished. They will summon help from the Sun City.'

Elin smiled. 'And word of our attack will smoke the Catcher and the Weaver from the Sun City like foxes from their lair. They cannot allow Altara to fall. When they hear that Altara burns, they will ride to the warriors' aid and leave the city poorly defended.'

'Azbarak will be left to guard the gates.'

'The Keeper will not stand against me. I will take Caspia. We will ride and seize the palace,' Elin's eyes flashed. 'And take the sun-stone.'

She looked at Caspia. Her eyes narrowed. 'And if you are strong enough daughter, I will make you Sun Catcher and Queen after me.'

Caspia's heart leapt. 'I am strong, Mother!'

She quelled the whisper of doubt. The silk hadn't sung for her. She shook off the feeling. She hadn't set herself a true test. Not given the silk a chance to know her. Not prepared herself properly. She had been foolish to sneak into her mother's room, to hide in the shadows, to slip the silk from the travel-stained bag and pull on the coat. Foolish to expect the creased cloth to sing in the gloom of the cold, stone room. The coat needed light so that the tiny crystals sparkled and the silk gleamed. Of course it would stay still and silent until it was taken to the sun hall.

'You will need to be, daughter. You will have to take the stone. The imposter who calls herself the Sun Catcher won't give it to you.' Elin frowned. 'She's cunning. She tricked me. Kept me from taking back the stone. She used the silk against me.'

Her fingers crawled across her dress. Her face twisted as she fought to control them, to stop them touching the water-stained silk patches sewn to her gown. Her hands curled into fists. 'Used my sisters' voices against me.'

Her body shuddered. 'You are weaker,' she hissed. 'I will not hear you.' She drummed her fists against the hewn log she sat on. 'Your voices are drowning in the lake. I cannot hear you!'

Urteth pulled her to her feet. 'Our daughter will be strong. As you are strong. She will wear the silk and the sun-helmet. You will make her Queen.'

Elin lifted her shaking hand to touch the raw burn which scarred his cheek.

Caspia could not bear to watch the gentle gesture. Could not witness her mother's pain, her father's hurt.

'We are strong together,' she said. 'And we will destroy the usurper who tries to harm us.'

CHAPTER SIX

Elin had ordered the torches to be lit in the great hall.
Fingers of soot from the flames streaked the stones.
Light glinted off the bronze links of Wulf Kin breastplates.
The fire threw giant shadows into the corners, stretching the
shapes of eagles and wulfen into huge, distorted creatures
that flickered across the walls. A night-wake army prowling
through the mountain stronghold. An army ready to unleash
its fury against the warriors at Altara. To hunt down Maia, the
usurper Sun Catcher. To put their Queen and her daughter
in her place.

Caspia walked towards the dais at the far end of the
hall. The Wulf Kin moved aside to let her pass. She smiled,
stealing their thoughts. They would follow her.

She mounted the shallow steps where her father and
mother sat in tall carved chairs. The third painted and gilded

34

chair was empty. It was hers to claim. No longer would she sit at Elin's feet. She would stand at her side. Her mother would make her Sun Catcher and heir.

Silk tumbled from the empty seat; the tiny crystals sewn into the coat glimmered like stars. The story-coat. It was hers to wear. Her mother couldn't listen to its stories. She hated the silk. It tormented her with tales of the has-been.

The coat held the stories and secrets of Khandar. The silk's knowledge made the Story Singer all-powerful. As strong as the Queen. As dangerous as the Sun Catcher. With stone, silk and gold, she, Caspia, daughter of Urteth the Eagle Hunter and Elin, the red witch, would become the greatest ruler of all. All she needed was the sun-stone. And Elin and Urteth had promised they would seize the stone from the Sun City and remove Maia and Tareth, the Warrior Weaver, before the snowfalls of wolf-walk.

In the golden fire-glare, Urteth's face was dark, the scars no longer visible. Caspia wondered if that was why her mother had filled the hall with shifting light and shadows. Urteth commanded the Wulf Kin. He needed to be strong. The Wulf Kin's loyalty was only given to those whose will and strength were greater than their own. And Urteth's strength had been diminished. The sun-stone had burned him. Maia the imposter had tricked him into holding the stone when the sunlight blazed into the crystal. It had crippled his hand. Taken his right eye. Remade his face so that he was not the father she remembered, but one who burned with anger and blinked away from sunlight and firelight.

She saw him glance at Elin and look away. Her mother's fingers were bright with jewels, her hands curved round a golden helmet. The Sun Catcher helmet Elin had spirited away from the Sun City. She would place the gleaming headpiece on her daughter's head when she regained the throne.

Caspia smiled at Urteth, trying not to notice how his scars twisted, looking instead at the black wolf pelt bristling across his shoulders and then at the restless young eagle hunched on the arm of his chair. Half-tame, half-wild, the bird was little comfort for her father who still mourned Azara, the bird killed by the Warrior Women. Caspia promised herself again that all would suffer for his loss.

She bowed her head as she stood before Elin, waiting as her mother brushed her cold lips across her forehead.

'Stand tall, daughter,' murmured Elin.

The silk sighed when the long skirt of her dress brushed against it as she reached her chair. This time it would sing to her. Caspia realised that she had been holding her breath. It was going to be all right. Here, now, it would accept her. Would let her wear it when her mother placed the helmet on her head. After all, this was a story the coat wanted. The coat was always worn for sun-catching and for crowning. And Elin would crown her Queen-to-be here in the Tower of Eagles.

Caspia faced the crowded hall. She could see Zartev, the old Wulf Kin who had saved her father from the stone fire. He stood tall and still to the side of the dais within a knife thrust of Urteth. If only he had ridden with her father when he had followed the Sun Catcher. He had arrived too late to kill the girl. Beside him Vultek rested his hand on the hilt of his knife.

Caspia probed his thoughts. She hid a smirk. Vultek was

greedy. He was thinking of the feast which would follow. She could smell roast meats. Hot beer. Her favourite honey breads. She threw her thought-stealing nets wide. The Wulf Kin would support her claim and fight by her side.

Elin rose, raised her arms, holding the polished helmet high.

'The sun-helmet of my family,' she called, her voice carrying above the swell of sound in the solar. 'It is returned to the true heir.'

Caspia felt her father rise and stand beside her. Saw him lift the silk coat from the painted chair.

'The silk of the Story Singer,' cried Elin. 'The story-coat is returned. We give them to our daughter Caspia that she may stand as Sun Catcher, and Queen-to-be.'

The Wulf Kin howled. Their wulfen bayed. The sound sent shivers across Caspia's skin. Urteth hung the silk about her, his hands squeezing her shoulders as he stepped back. Caspia realised with a jolt that Elin was too afraid to handle the coat herself.

She slipped her arms into the long sleeves. The cool silk fell over her hands. She held her arms wide and saw the crystals shimmer. Felt the silk sigh, heard the whisper, 'Sun Catcher'. And glimpsed a girl with red hair wearing the coat, waiting to receive the helmet. She saw herself. And the dark man with an eagle feather in his hair and the face of her father lifting the helmet. Yet not her father. He didn't wear a black wolfskin slung from his shoulders. His face wasn't scarred. She gasped. The girl was not her. The image faded. The silk was silent.

Elin stepped forward. She raised the sun-helmet. The

Wulf Kin roared. Pulling their knives from their sheaths they beat them on the bronze discs of their chest armour.

'Caspia, your future Queen,' proclaimed Elin.

'Caspia!' They were like the bellow of the wind through ice-locked valleys.

Their thoughts battered her. Thrilling her with their loyalty. Her heart leapt. She was theirs. They were hers. She reached out to find and catch their exultant joy.

Elin placed the helmet on her head.

The sudden silence deafened her. Her sight deserted her. She tried to cast her thought-stealing net. It was too heavy to throw. It slipped from her. She swayed. Blindly she lowered her hands to grab the silk, rubbing it between her fingers, desperate to hear it murmur. Nothing.

The coat and the helmet made her nothing. They robbed her of her gift. They would not acknowledge her as Queen. They remembered the red-haired girl. They chose her. While Maia lived, she, Caspia, was nothing.

Caspia felt Elin seize her hand, hold her arm high. She sensed that Urteth had stepped close to her and lifted her other arm in triumph. The Wulf Kin must be cheering. She could feel the vibration of their pounding feet through the soles of her boots. She held tight to her parents' hands. If they let go she would fall.

Her knees sagged. She fought to keep her head high.

The weight of the helmet pressed down on her. The silk was listening, draining all warmth from her. There was nothing for it to hear. Her mind was numb, images erased, her thoughts washed away. She had to escape the coat, drag off the helmet before she fell.

She managed to turn her head. Through the silk eyepieces she could just see Elin. Her face rippled as if she was underwater. Her lips moved. Caspia gripped hard, digging her nails into her mother's flesh. Urteth slackened his hold and she clawed at his hand.

She felt his intake of breath and the power that surged through him. Knew he was bellowing her name, inciting the Wulf Kin. She tried to hold on, draw in some of his strength.

Then she was swung away, pulled behind the tall chairs, and the helmet pushed from her head.

She gasped with relief.

'What is it?' Elin demanded.

Caspia shivered, shrugging herself out of the silk. Urteth caught it as it slid from her shoulders.

'Nothing,' said Caspia shakily. 'There was nothing.'

'Nothing?' repeated Elin. 'Listen to them roar. They are waiting for you. You are to be their Queen.'

'I am no one,' said Caspia. 'The daughter of exiles.' She shook. 'Less than nothing.'

Elin's eyes flashed. 'You wore the helmet. And the silk. How can that be nothing? You cannot weaken now!'

Caspia flinched and looked to Urteth. He was kinder than her mother.

'Enough of this,' Urteth growled. 'You are the daughter of a queen. You will go back to the hall. Smile. Sit and feast.

39

Behave like the heir to your family's power. Don't cower here like a whimpering child.'

His scorn was worse than Elin's. Caspia tossed back her hair, drew herself up and glowered at him. She was as strong as he was.

'I'm not a child.' She flung out her hand. It still trembled, but at least the chill of the silk was fading. It was good to be angry. It warmed her. Reminded her who she was. 'The Wulf Kin will follow me. Listen to them. They don't follow a child.'

Urteth softened. 'So be strong. Show them.' He held out the coat.

'Wear it and walk among them as Queen. Let the feasting begin. Come.'

He shook the coat. The silk was dull. It hung limp and silent. The crystals were dim. Yet it listened. She knew it sensed her despair. She hated it for making her feel lost and afraid.

Caspia stepped away from him, twitching her long skirts so that they didn't touch the silk. 'The coat doesn't sing for me.'

'What are you saying, daughter?' demanded Elin. 'Put on the silk!'

'I can't wear it. I won't.' She clenched her fists. 'I don't need the silk to show what I am. You didn't wear the coat, yet you were Queen.'

Elin's eyes narrowed. 'The future Queen wears the silk and the helmet when she is proclaimed heir – and when she is crowned. Stone, silk, gold. That is what we hold. What you must hold when they call you Queen.'

'You didn't,' said Caspia, risking her mother's wrath. 'The

40

stone was hidden. The silk gone. You didn't lay claim to silk, stone and gold. Yet you called yourself Queen.'

'I was the eldest daughter. It was my right to reign as Queen and Catcher,' retorted Elin. 'And I will reign again! You are my daughter. You will be Queen. Put on the helmet and the coat and show them what you are.'

'What use is the helmet or the coat if I cannot hold the stone?' Caspia looked at her father. 'How can I be Queen while the Sun Catcher keeps the sun-stone in the Sun City and rules Khandar?'

Elin's face twisted. She clutched the silk band woven into the front of her gown. 'Are you making me a liar, daughter? Haven't I just made you Queen-to-be? Was I mistaken? Will you allow the usurper to take your place? Crawl back to the Sun Palace to return the silk and gold I stole for you?'

Caspia bit her lip. She had gone too far. No one dared speak of the has-been when her mother had seized the throne from the ashes of her sisters' deaths.

'No, Mother.'

Elin's fingers stroked the silk strip at her waist, her nails rasping against the worn threads. It seemed to calm her. She sighed. 'What happened when you wore the silk. When you put on the sun-helmet?'

Caspia stared at the toes of her boots. She noticed how worn the leather had become. They were not the boots of a queen. The silk had known she was not a queen-to-be. 'It called out: Sun Catcher.'

'Yes! I told you it was the to-come,' Elin shot a look of triumph at Urteth. 'When we return to the Sun City, Caspia will be Sun Catcher of Khandar.'

'It whispered Sun Catcher,' continued Caspia, willing her mother to be silent and listen. 'And showed me a man who looked like my father, placing the helmet on my head. But it was not me, nor my father.' She glanced at Urteth. He looked puzzled, then his face grew pale with anger, although his scars burned red.

'Tareth!' he muttered.

'And then there was nothing. Silence. Emptiness. Darkness. I couldn't hear anything. I was blind and deaf and dumb.' She turned to Elin. 'The helmet stole my thoughts. The silk knew. It knew I wasn't the true Queen.

'I will never wear the silk, nor the helmet, not while the girl Maia lives.' She bit her lip. 'She found the hidden stone. She is the Queen.'

'Never!' hissed Elin.

'She has claimed the gold and silk. They are hers, not mine.'

'Then she will not live to wear them.' Elin snatched up the bag lying behind Urteth's seat and thrust it at him. 'Put it away.'

She watched him stuff the coat into the bag, then placed the helmet at the foot of the chair.

'The Wulf Kin saw our daughter in the helmet and the silk. That must be enough until we have dealt with the imposter. Summon the old one. Zartev must hide them away. He is loyal. He will tell no one what has happened here.' Her eyes were cold as she looked at Caspia. 'We will never speak of this again. Urteth will send Wulf Kin to seek out the girl. The silk will sing for you when she is dead.'

Urteth toed the bag under his chair. 'I will send eagles with them.'

'And when she is with her sisters, nothing will stand in our way – in *your* way,' said Elin.

She smoothed her hand over Caspia's long red hair, and tugged the sleeves down to cover her wrists. She slipped a ring from her finger and pushed it on Caspia's thumb.

'Take Urteth's arm. He will lead you among the Wulf Kin. Stand tall. Let the light fall on your hand. The jewel will blaze in the torchlight. You will look like a true heir to my throne.'

'Come,' said Urteth. The wolfskin across his shoulders bristled, making him seem broader and taller than he was. Caspia put her hand on his arm and admired the stone on her thumb. A flame burned deep in the heart of the jewel. Red for fire. Red for anger.

She smiled. Her mother's jewel was as red as the crests of the little colour-shifting lizards Vultek had trapped for her. She didn't need the Wulf Kin to seek out the Sun Catcher. She knew how to find her. The boy who loved lizards would show her. The boy who had promised to get her silk. All she had to do was to find him.

Holding her father's arm, she walked out among the Wulf Kin. They still shouted her name. But all she heard was the pounding of feet. The drumming of their knives on bronze. It beat out the rhythm of a name.

Kodo. Kodo.

CHAPTER SEVEN

Maia knew that Kodo was upset. She was troubled too. She had thought that the Watcher and her crows would go with them across the Vast. She needed her wisdom, her knowledge of the grasslands, her ability to track and forage and fight if needed. Her birds would have warned her of any danger. Now they must rely on Var.

She watched the black rat nibbling a nut that Var had found, and crumbled the last of the stale flatbread Kodo had shared with her and scattered it on the ground for the red-legged crow strutting in front of her. Nefrar's nose twitched as the bird bobbed. He snorted and its feathers stood on end.

Maia laughed. She held out her hand and the bird flew to her. Its claws pricked her skin as it balanced on her forefinger. It stared at her, cocking its head, its eyes bright. At least this bird wasn't afraid of her. She pushed aside thoughts of the young eagle she had hurt. Tareth would have healed KiKya by now. The silk she had left would have helped. And now she carried cocoons in her back-sack. Tareth could tease new silk from those. She touched the bag, checking that it was securely fastened. She must keep it safe. It was the last of the silk from the moth-garden. There were no more cocoons.

'Kodo. Var,' she called. They joined her.

'We must decide what to do now that the Watcher has left us,' she said.

Kodo bristled. Var watched her, his eyes thoughtful.

'The Watcher told you the waymarkers to seek,' said Maia. 'You must tell us. Kodo is a skilled way-finder. Trader trusted him to steer his ship. There are few signs to follow across the sun-deeps yet he kept a true wave-track.'

'I find the way using wind and waves,' said Kodo. 'The wind blows here.' He gestured to a tumble of large stones and the distant swell of grasslands. 'And there are markers and waves too. I can find our way.'

Maia nodded.

'Well?' Kodo glared at Var. 'Tell us what she said,' he demanded.

Var was silent. He gave Tiki another nut.

'The Watcher made you our guide. But if we're separated, each of us must know the way,' said Maia.

Var shrugged. 'She told me the stars to find. The shadow to mark at sun-wake. I will show you.' He looked at Kodo. 'And you. So even you cannot get lost.'

Maia grabbed Kodo's arm to stop him retaliating. 'We must travel swiftly. There are many dangers. The Wulf Kin hunt across the Vast.' She shivered. 'We should watch for the

People of the Running Horses who follow their herds far and wide across the Vast. Then we could ride to Khandar.'

Kodo looked over the empty grasslands. 'Where will they be?'

Maia frowned. 'They move with their horses. When Yanna and I found them beyond Altara they had made stone walls to keep their horses and sheep safe from wolves. Now they will be in their solstice pastures until the snows come. They will need to be close to water. So we must find a lake . . . Or a river.'

'How?' asked Kodo. No one from the cliffs or the Stilt Village ever went to the Vast.

'Birds need to drink. They will fly to water,' said Var. He looked at the crow. 'There will be trees.'

'And clouds,' said Kodo. 'When the land is hot, open water makes clouds.'

Maia studied the cloudless sky. 'The horses may be far from our way. We might never find them.'

Kodo looked back at the purple smudge that was all that they could see of the hills. Beyond it lay home. And the sun-deeps.

'We could go back, find Trader, travel with him. He would take us to Haddra and then to the Sun City.'

Maia shook her head. 'We might never find the ship. And the Marsh Lord's holdfast overlooks the sun-deeps.'

Var strapped on his running blades. 'I can go faster alone. I will seek the horse herds. If I cannot find them it will be safer to leave the Vast. It's too open.' He squinted at the sun, turned and raised his arm. 'You should move along the shadow. Then find the Dog Star and walk towards it. I will find you.'

Kodo watched him stride away. His pace lengthened and then he was running, bounding through the grass.

'How d'we know he's looking for horses? He could be summoning the Marsh Lord. Laying a trail for his hounds. Then we will be easy to find.'

Maia slung the back-sack over her shoulder. 'The Watcher trusts him. So should we. Come.'

Var returned alone as the sun sank below the horizon and shadows streaked the sky. He moved so silently that Maia jumped as he halted beside her.

'You have done well and come far,' he said. He removed his running blades and knelt to catch Tiki. 'I caught a grasscock.' Var pulled a plump brown bird with yellow legs from his pack. 'It will make good eating.'

'And Kodo dug some roots and found dung for fuel.' Maia slipped off her own back-sack, glad to have stopped jogging. 'It's old and dry. Horses must have passed this way.' She took her fire makings from her belt pouch. 'If we are alone we can light a fire. Have a feast.'

'I saw no one,' Var said. He didn't say that the silence and emptiness of the grasslands had seemed ominous. He thought about telling them he had found the skeleton of a dead pony. The bones had been crushed and gnawed. It was an old kill. But fierce beasts had hunted here. He had searched but found no tracks.

'Good.' Kodo took the bird from Var and began plucking it. 'A pity you didn't catch lapran too.'

But his thoughts were less harsh as he sat, fat shining on his chin, gnawing on a plump leg of cooked grasscock. He raked a baked tuber from the ashes and split it open to scoop out the steaming white pulp. 'All we need is flatbread and chay.'

Maia licked her greasy fingers. 'Blueberry flatbreads.'

Nefrar, his whiskers bloodied from a kill, padded towards the fire and stretched out beside her.

'So you've eaten too.' She watched him clean his fur. 'We'll need to find water soon.' Like them, Nefrar had chewed the roots of raingrass, sucking moisture from the tiny swollen bulbs, but the big cat needed more water than they did. She pulled up a stem, stripped off the tiny bulbs and fed them to Nefrar.

Kodo lay back and stared at the stars which were beginning to wink above them.

Maia glanced at Var then stared into the darkness. 'If we cannot find the People of the Running Horses then we must look for the quickest way to the Sun City.' She checked that her back-sack was close. It seemed to have grown heavier. She wondered if the silk was listening to the silence of the plains and sensing her disquiet.

'We should go to the sun-deeps. Find a boat,' said Kodo.

Var ignored him. 'There is another way. There will be danger. But no one will follow. No one will enter the sands at the edge of the Hidden.'

'Cross the Hidden?'

'No!' yelled Kodo. He hurled the bone he had been chewing. It thudded into Maia's sack. Var's black rat scuttled away. 'Get off, thief!' he roared. He grabbed a stone and flung it after the rat. 'Keep him off,' he said fiercely. 'Or I'll smash his skull.' He glared at Maia. 'Tell him to get rid of it, or I will. The rat's a thief, not to be trusted. Like its master.'

Maia pulled her back-sack closer. The drawstring was loose. She tugged it tight and pushed the bag beneath her knees.

'There's no food in my sack. We've eaten it all.'

Kodo's eyes narrowed. The rat could destroy the silk cocoons. Eat the moth eggs. He felt for his knife and thought he heard the silk hidden beneath it whisper. The silk feared the rat too.

'How can we cross the Hidden with a rat thief?' he argued. 'How can we trust its master, an assassin to find the way across? The Hidden is like a lizard scrape. Hot. Dry. Sand and rocks. We'll starve if we don't die of thirst. '

'There is food and water there.' Var looked at Kodo. 'And even a way to the sun-deeps which lie beyond the Hidden,' he said.

'How d'you know?' asked Maia.

Var watched Tiki creeping from the shadows. He held out his hand and the rat leapt onto his palm. He stroked his whiskers.

'He doesn't know,' scoffed Kodo.

'I was found in the Hidden,' Var said. 'I can take you to the people of the sands. They will guide us across the dunes.' The lie tasted bitter on his tongue. The Hidden kept its secrets. He might not find the people who lived there. But these open plains weren't safe. He knew that danger lurked in the grasslands. He had felt it like feathers brushing his skin. He wished he had the far sight of a bird.

'It's a way to the Sun City. If you need it,' he said.

The windblown sand stung his skin, blinded him, filled his mouth. If there had been any moisture left on his tongue Kodo would have spat out the grit and dirt. He tugged the band of cloth Maia had given him up over his chin and mouth and shut his eyes. The wind had come suddenly. He had been watching long strings of sand blowing like torn banners from the top of the red ochre dunes. Then a flying frenzy attacked.

When darkness fell, cold fogs rolled in. Fogs that covered them with drops of moisture that Var had told them to lick up to quench their thirst. Var had even shown them how to dig a hollow to collect the dew on a cloth so that they had a mouthful of water to drink come sunrise. He knew how to survive in this land that baked them in the day and made them shiver in the darkness. They would have died here without him.

He slid down the dune and fell over Nefrar who was sheltering from the wind. Maia joined him. They huddled together, stunned into silence, sucking air through the cloths they had tied over their mouths as the sand piled against them. Nefrar struggled to his feet, head bowed, tail to the wind. He looked as miserable as Kodo felt. Nothing could live here. The Watcher's red-legged crow had disappeared.

Kodo wondered if it was dead. He hoped the bird had flown back to its home on the cliffs.

Var tugged his arm then pushed a small lump into his hand.

'Chew it.' Var's voice was torn away by the wind. He put a seed pod in his own mouth, handing Maia another. Kodo spat out sand and chewed. His mouth was filled with bittersweet saliva. He almost smiled with relief.

When the wind died, they dug themselves out from the small dune which had formed round them and shook the sand from their clothes. Nefrar grunted and heaved himself up.

Maia ran her palm across her face. Sand scratched her skin.

Crawling on hands and knees she scaled the dune they had sheltered behind and peered across the folds and waves of the landscape. The sand glistened. She thought she saw smooth grey mounds in the distance. A lone thorn tree stuck out of the sand like a cluster of abandoned spears.

Maia pointed. 'I can see something. A tree. Huge rocks.'

Var nodded. 'There may be water.'

Kodo slid down the dune. 'Come then,' he said wearily and trudged after Var.

CHAPTER EIGHT

Tareth watched his eagle KiKya as she drank. Her wing looked stronger. He would pour water in a shallow bowl and let her bathe. A palace boy skirted the eagle and placed the bundle of spun thread beside them. He had never seen the boy before. Since Azbarak's return to the city, there seemed to be more children in the palace. He would speak to the Keeper. There were better things for children to be doing than fetching and carrying and tending the palace fires.

'Will make beautiful cloth, master.'

Zena fingered the bright saffron yarn. She held it against the hanks of blue wool she had piled on the stone floor.

Tareth smiled. Zena was an apt pupil. She still tired easily after Elin's attack, but she was becoming a skilled weaver, eager to learn, her fingers swift, her eye for colour sure. He wondered if he would dare to teach her to weave silk. Would she be safe from its song? Maia had told him how Zena had carried the story-coat from Altara when she had followed her to the Sun City. She had not been afraid of the silk. When Maia returned with the cocoons he would ask Zena to help in the new moth-garden. The silk would show him if his instincts were right.

KiKya lurched clumsily and perched on the arm of the tall chair. Soon she would be ready to fly. He touched the silk strip binding her injury. It was silent. It was Maia's silk. Silk woven beside the sun-deeps. Silk which had never sung. But it felt warm beneath his fingertips. He whispered to it, but the silk did not respond. Maia didn't trust it. She hadn't remembered that silk could heal as well as ensnare. If she had, perhaps Xania would have lived. In his attempt to protect her, he'd kept the secrets of her past and the marvels of the material from her.

At Maia's Naming, the Watcher had accused him of failing, of letting Maia discover her gift without guidance. He had placed Maia in danger then. He had done so again. He needed silk. He must weave. He had no choice. He clenched his fists. He had given in to the demands of the silk. He had sent her back to the Cliff Village, with only Razek and Kodo to aid her. He should have gone with them.

He watched Zena setting the coloured threads side by side, choosing which to weave together. Would he endanger her too? Perhaps he shouldn't expect Zena to follow him. But there must be a new weaver, and Maia had no sisters left to weave for her.

The palace boy was almost knocked over by Yanna as she strode into the room. The archer glared as he scuttled away.

'Azbarak's urchins are everywhere. They scurry like rats. Hide in corners. Bring him news from the market place. And beyond.'

'Is there news of Maia?' asked Tareth.

Yanna shook her head. 'Rumours only that the Sun Catcher has left the city.' She fingered the plaited braid knotted around her wrist and frowned. 'She would need eagle wings to have crossed the Vast and returned already.'

'She went across the sun-deeps with Trader.'

'And so must wait for good winds,' said Yanna. 'Leaf-fall will turn to wolf-walk before we can expect her. If the snows come before she does, the city will be fearful. They will remember the hunger and long cold when Elin was Queen. We need the Catcher to bring down the last of the sun before the dark and cold.'

'She will be here,' promised Tareth. 'The harvest is good. Azbarak has filled the granaries.'

Yanna grunted and twisted the coloured band.

'What is it?' asked Tareth.

Yanna stared at KiKya. 'There has been no word from Altara.'

'None?' asked Tareth, surprised.

'Do you trust Azbarak, the Keeper?' demanded Yanna.

Tareth was quiet. 'He serves the Sun Catcher,' he said.

'He served Elin too,' stated Yanna. 'He changes his coat easily.'

Tareth's eyes danced. 'He has many fine coats,' he agreed, thinking of the magnificently embroidered clothing the Keeper wore.

Yanna scowled.

Tareth hid his smile. 'Shall I ask Zena to weave you a coat so you can strut like our Keeper?'

Yanna's expression softened as she glanced at the bald-headed girl hanging weights on her loom.

'You are teaching her well, Weaver. We will make good use of her when we return to Altara. The Warrior Women will wear many colours.'

'I hoped that Zena would stay here, in the palace,' admitted Tareth. 'Maia has lost many friends.'

'You don't expect the lizard boy and the Storm Chaser to return with her?'

Tareth looked sombre. 'Their paths lie elsewhere,' he said. 'The role of a Sun Catcher is a solitary one. But Zena is loyal to Maia.'

Zena looked up. 'Lady come soon,' she said.

'Has there been a message?' Azbarak stepped forward.

For a large man the Keeper was as light on his feet as a cat, thought Tareth, wondering how long the man had been there, unseen, listening. He chided himself for his suspicion. He was letting Yanna's discontent darken his own thoughts.

'None. Haven't your urchin rats brought you gossip from the market?' retorted Yanna.

Azbarak flicked his fingers in greeting. 'Warrior. I did not see you there in the shadows.' He turned to Tareth. 'An eagle comes.'

'An eagle?' Tareth struggled to his feet. KiKya raised her wings to keep her balance.

'Gently little one,' Tareth soothed as he lowered his arm so that she could step onto the back of his chair. He waited until she had settled and turned to Azbarak.

'An eagle?' he repeated. 'A message? From Maia?'

Azbarak glanced sideways at Yanna. 'I am told the eagle flies from the mountains.'

Tareth stifled his disappointment. 'Not from Maia. She won't come through the mountains.' He swung from the room, hurrying towards the stone stairs spiralling inside the tower.

'Nor news from Altara,' said Yanna thoughtfully. 'The warriors would send a cheetah not an eagle.'

The bird allowed Tareth to detach the leather pouch tied to its leg.

'The Eagle People have sent it,' he said as he pulled a twisted cord from the pouch, his fingers busy decoding the knotted message.

A brightly plaited braid fluttered to the ground. Yanna seized it. 'I know this. It's Bekta's braid,' she exclaimed. 'Our youngest warrior.'

She looked at Tareth, her eyes wide with alarm. 'What does this mean? Why does an eagle bring her bow braid to you?'

Tareth held out a knotted loop. 'A hunter found this around the cheetah's neck.' He looked towards the mountains. 'In the snow-melt. In the river.' His gaze rested on Yanna. 'There was a cat. And a girl.'

'Alive?'

Tareth shook his head. 'The girl was dead. The cat dying.'

Yanna bit back a groan.

'They fell crossing a gorge. The hunter hid them beneath a cairn to protect them from scavengers and told Egon and the Eagle Hunters. Egon sent this to us.'

Yanna's fingers slid across the knots. 'Altara!' she said.

'Altara?' echoed Tareth.

Yanna's fist clenched around the knotted rope and brightly coloured braid. 'It has been attacked. The girl escaped to warn us. Altara is beseiged by Wulf Kin!'

CHAPTER NINE

'I must go. And I must take my archers with me.' Yanna spun on her heel to hurry from the tower. She paused, her face creased with anxiety. 'It will leave you and the city unguarded.'

Tareth watched as the eagle launched itself and flew steadily towards the distant mountains. 'Egon will have summoned the Eagle People. They will already be riding to Altara. Urteth's Wulf Kin cannot stand against eagles and warriors.'

'I cannot spare archers.'

'No need. You will have another warrior. I ride with you.' He felt his spirits rise. It would be good not to wait within the city walls searching the passes for Maia's return.

'The city needs you,' protested Yanna, even though her eyes gleamed at his offer.

'Azbarak can guard the city. The walls are high. The gates

are strong. It will be safe enough while Urteth and the Wulf Kin attack Altara.'

Tareth beckoned a boy squatting in the sunshine, tossing smooth stones from hand to hand.

'Find the Keeper. Bring him to the solar. Then seek out the Warrior Women and send them there too.'

The child nodded and scurried away.

A girl took his place. Taking a handful of round stones from her tunic she made a small pile next to herself. Then she pulled out a slingshot.

'Perhaps the city will not be unguarded after all,' said Yanna grimly. 'You have an army of urchins. Azbarak's orphan rats.'

'I need a horse, a bow and spears,' Tareth ordered as soon as Azbarak appeared. 'And food. For myself and the archers. The Warrior Women are leaving. I shall go with them. We ride for Altara. Wulf Kin have attacked the stronghold.'

'Aiee!' moaned Azbarak. He threw up his hands. 'It was a mistake to let Elin escape from the palace. She wishes to destroy the archers who followed the Catcher. She'll burn Altara to the ground.'

Tareth's eyes narrowed. 'You think Elin commands the Wulf Kin. That she has attacked Altara?'

'The Wulf Kin are Urteth's. He is a great warrior. And he does as Elin wishes. She will have gone to the Tower of Eagles to join him. Altara will fall. It is foolish to ride into danger, Weaver. We must wait in the city. Prepare to defend it. The Warrior Women should stay to defend the palace.'

'Altara will not fall. And you will remain in the city. I leave it in your care until the Catcher returns.'

Azbarak twisted the rings on his fingers. 'You have news

of the Catcher's return?'

'I expect none yet, but she will return before wolf-walk. The eagles will watch for her. I have asked the Eagle People to send word. You will hear when she is close.'

'The people will be glad when the Catcher returns. They believe they are safe when she is here.'

Tareth frowned. 'They are safe. Maia returned the sun-stone to the Sun City. She will catch the sun again.'

'She is not here,' said Azbarak softly.

'She has promised to return.'

'She is young and untried.'

'Untried? She found the stone. She caught the sun!' Tareth kept a tight rein on his temper. 'And though young, she understands what she must do. She is strong. Do you doubt her strength, Keeper?'

Azbarak shook his head. 'The stories tell us that all Catchers are strong.'

'It would be well to remember that the stories are true. And to remember that Elin fears her sister's power. A power that overcame her.'

Azbarak nodded. 'I saw her fear. I saw her silk madness. I witnessed the sun-catch and heard the people shout for their new Catcher as she held up the stone and caught the sun.'

'And Maia will return soon bringing a great gift to the Sun City. The moths will dance again in the palace garden. I will weave new silk for her. There will be a new Story Singer. Khandar will prosper. Maia will be a good queen.'

'It is what we all hope for,' said Azbarak.

'What we all know,' insisted Tareth. 'It is written in the stones.'

Azbarak lowered his eyes and studied the toes of his soft boots.

'Since that is so, I will do as you ask, Weaver, although I think you are unwise to leave with the Warrior Women.'

'Altara protected Maia when I could not. She would have died in the Vast if they hadn't found her. I owe them her life. I will defend their stronghold now.'

Azbarak shrugged. 'Then I will wait for the Catcher. I will keep the Sun City safe and greet you at the city gates when you have saved Altara.'

Tareth ignored the barb in Azbarak's reply. 'I leave the city in your care, Keeper. Guard it well until Maia or I return.'

'What if the city is attacked before the Catcher comes? If Urteth and the Wulf Kin descend like howling wolves I have no archers to defend the city. Only walls and gates.'

Tareth met the fat man's bland gaze. With the storeroom of weapons Elin and Urteth had left in the palace, Azbarak could muster and arm a ragtag fighting force if he needed. Surely there would be traders and citizens prepared to resist any threat to the city? And there should be enough stores in the granary to withstand a short siege. He doubted the wisdom of leaving Azbarak in charge. But he owed a debt to Yanna. And defeating the Wulf Kin at Altara would protect the city.

He sighed and made his decision.

'Should I fail and Urteth bring the Wulf Kin, you must do what you think is best for the people of the city.

Azbarak bowed his head. 'Yes, Weaver.'

'Warrior Weaver,' snapped Yanna as she strode into the solar.

Azbarak's bow deepened. 'Warrior Weaver,' he said.

Yanna watched as Tareth encouraged KiKya onto his fist. 'The eagle rides with you?'

Tareth glanced at Azbarak. 'I cannot ask Keeper to care for her. She answers only to me.' He saw the fat man's sigh of relief. 'I must return her to the wild before she is fit to hunt for herself or she must take her chances and come into danger with me.'

He stroked the eagle's breast. KiKya leaned forward and nudged his cheek with her beak. Tareth smiled. 'She has chosen. She comes with me.'

'And she will fall like an arrow from the sky on the Wulf Kin who dare attack Altara,' promised Yanna. She raised her fist to salute the young eagle. 'KiKya, Sky Warrior!'

'Sky Warrior!' proclaimed Tareth.

KiKya clumsily stretched out her injured wing, and screamed a challenge as if the solar were besieged by foes.

CHAPTER TEN

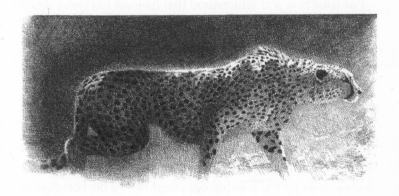

Maia's chin dropped to her chest. She jerked awake. She had to watch over Kodo. Had to make sure that Tiki didn't nibble his way into her back-sack. He was hungry. They all were. She hoped Var would hunt successfully. She yawned. The cold was making her drowsy. She wouldn't have believed that a land that could be so hot in the sun could be bitter cold once darkness fell. Or that somewhere that seemed so empty and dry could support life – some of it deadly.

She shivered, remembering the fight Var and Kodo had had when Kodo had collected dried seed pods from a dead bush and cut its roots to burn on the fire. Var had shouted that Kodo would kill them all – that if they slept by a fire made from the deadly roots they would not wake with sunrise. That everyone knew that the claw tree leached a deadly sap. When Kodo had thrown the seed pods to Tiki to nibble, Var had felled him with a single blow. Spitting with rage, he threatened to feed Kodo the deadly seeds if he ever tried to harm the rat.

At least now Var understood that he must tell them about this place of many perils. And the hot, sand-covered land had become fascinating. Even Kodo had listened as Var explained the meaning of the strange marks they found in the sand: the parallel whip marks of a sidewinding snake; the splayed feet of long-striding birds that couldn't fly; the prints of a lone deer that Var said had long thin horns and a black and white face. Prints and dung were all they had seen. Dung that moved. They had stared and seen beetles rolling balls of it away. He pointed out a high-flying bird carrying a writhing snake in its beak. Maia's heart had leapt when she saw it was an eagle. She had thought that it was searching for her, that Tareth or the Eagle People were watching for her return. But it had been wild. A black-breasted snake eagle, swallowing its prey.

Later Var had shown her how to wear his running blades. She had staggered and fallen on her face when she tried to stride out. He had laughed and let her practise until she could walk without falling.

But Kodo had refused to try the running blades. He didn't like Var. He didn't like the Hidden. Maia did. She loved the ever-changing scorched landscape: the low grasslands of the foothills on the edge of the Vast where flocks of tiny black and white birds stripped seed heads from the tall dry grasses; the long lines of red ochre dunes rolling like waves, shaped into hills, crescent moons and stars that told the story of the shifting winds that made them; the plains of glittering gravel speckled with tiny lichens that unfurled to drink the fog; even the dry stream beds where the water had worn away small crumbling mounds so that it felt as if she was walking between the broken walls of an ancient settlement that was once as crowded as the Sun City. Kodo was spooked by the place. He said he felt as if he was being watched by people from the has-been. He had walked quickly, exhausting himself so they could leave the dried up riverbed.

Maia loved the emptiness. She loved watching the mist being burned off by the sun. She felt at home as she never had by the watery sun-deeps or in the stone Sun City. But she knew it was a place of danger where spitting snakes could blind. The sun-wake before last they had heard the grunts of a distant beast. A lion, Var had said, a flesh-eater bigger than Nefrar.

Maia wriggled until she found a good place to rest her back. The humped grey rocks had been scored by sand and wind until they were ridged like the bones of the giant lizards Kodo rode. Soon she would wake him so he could watch. She rubbed her numb fingers, wondering if she should blow the embers in the shallow fire pit into flames and add a little more of their precious store of shredded bark. Firelight would guide Var back from his hunt.

A shadow moved. A tall figure towered over her. A figure on running blades.

'Var?'

In the red ember glow she saw long naked legs and the shaft of a spear. Another elongated shadow. And a third, moving silently towards the sleeping Nefrar. She kicked out to jolt Kodo awake and froze as she felt a wide sharp blade pressed against her ribs.

She heard Nefrar growl, saw him spring.

A man shouted as he fell beneath the cat.

She felt the spear tip shift from her side, as the figure stepped forward, lifting his weapon to stab Nefrar. Maia launched forward and sent him tumbling.

Kodo staggered through the embers. Maia tried to pin her spearman to the ground. Nefrar roared, a roar that ended in a grunt of pain.

Maia felt fear surge through her. Nefrar was hurt. Light and fire coiled round her, choking her. The figure she grappled with gasped as her hands scorched his shoulder. She rolled away, her hands outstretched, to save Nefrar. Her vision turned gold. A thunder of drums pounded behind her eyes.

'Stop! Stop! They are Kuma! Friends!'

Var sprang from the darkness. He dropped the snake he was carrying.

'Friends!' he yelled.

Maia turned blindly, straining to hear.

'Kuma! Sand People! Friends!' He wrestled with Kodo, pulling him away.

Maia drew in a shuddering breath. It tasted of fire. She folded her arms across her chest, hiding her shaking hands. She felt the bitter cold drain the heat from them until she was shivering from the chill of the desert.

'Friends?'

Var broke into a torrent of strange speech.

'Friend?' she said again.

'They have a home nearby. Water. Fire. Shelter. They'll share it with us. They have hunted. There will be a big meal. A feast.'

Maia glanced at Kodo. Food. And water. 'Thank you,' she said.

Nefrar's tail stopped twitching.

The leader pointed his spear at the cheetah.

'He won't harm you,' said Maia quickly.

Nefrar yawned and blinked at the man, then sat on Maia's foot.

Maia caught the glimmer of a surprised smile. Then the leader flicked his fingers in a gesture of greeting to her, the big cat and finally Var and Kodo. She touched her forehead with her fist and opened her palm in a sign of friendship and stared hard at Kodo until he did the same. She noticed Var mirror the hunter's silent greeting and let her hand drop away from her knife.

She bent to examine the small puncture wound on Nefrar's shoulder. It had stopped bleeding. When they reached the Kuma's home she would ask Var to find water and heal-leaf or whatever heal-fast they used for injuries.

Var picked up the dead snake and offered it to the tall, thin hunter. Taking it, he gestured at them to follow and the three men disappeared into the shadows.

'Come,' said Var.

'Where did they go?' asked Kodo. 'Did he say there was going to be a feast?'

They heard a soft bird call.

'This way,' urged Var. 'Follow quickly. They wear running blades. They'll move swiftly.'

He set off with Kodo close on his heels. Maia grabbed her back-sack, tossed sand over the dying embers and hurried after them.

CHAPTER ELEVEN

The arrival of the hunters, with the deer carcass carried on their shoulders, was greeted by excited cries. The chatter died as the nomads saw the three who followed.

Maia kept her hand firmly on Nefrar's shoulder as she strode through the cluster of sand-red people. They drew back as they saw the cheetah. She heard them mutter. Several of the tall sand-smeared men stooped to pick up their spears. She was glad when Var fell into step on the other side of the big cat and placed his hand beside hers. The tip of Nefrar's tail twitched. He swung his head from side to side, watching the startled nomads and when their leader stopped, he sat on Maia's foot and purred.

'Wise cat,' thought Maia, as the spears were lowered. She rubbed his head. Nefrar stared at a small boy standing by a fire pit. The stick he had been using to hook baked grubs started to smoke. Nefrar's rumble deepened. The boy twitched, pulled his burning stick from the fire and stabbed it into the sand without taking his eyes from the cat. Nefrar blinked several times. The boy's eyes widened until he looked like an owl. He swallowed nosily, pulled a face and blinked slowly at Nefrar. The cat flopped down and rolled over. The invitation to tickle his stomach was clear. The child stepped forward, ignoring the warning cry of the woman who had been painting her body with red clay scooped from a huge white shell.

Maia smiled as the boy crept towards them.

'He's friendly' she said. 'He won't bite.'

Her voice sounded loud. The boy jumped back, ready to take flight.

'He likes you.'

Encouraged by her grin the youngster reached out and touched Nefrar. The cat lay still. The boy crouched and pushed his fingers through the soft fur on Nefrar's chest. He was the colour of the desert, noticed Maia, his skin covered with a coating of grease and sand. Tiny grains of quartz reflected the sunlight, making him gleam. The body paint must protect him against the heat of the sun.

The boy chuckled as Nefrar rolled to his feet and lifted his paw so that he could hold it. Someone in the crowd chuckled. Maia felt the tension ease.

As the hunters lowered their kill, some of them crowded to examine it. They gave Maia and the cheetah a wide berth, staring, wide-eyed and curious.

'At sundown they will feast.' Var took the eggshell from the boy and drank, mopping a dribble from his chin with the back of his hand. 'Dancing. And a feast.'

'But not until sun-sleep?' said Kodo, his voice as hollow as his stomach.

A woman laughed. She spoke to her child. He scampered to the fire, stirred the ashes and flipped small brown pellets from the flames. Blowing on his fingers he picked them up and dropped them onto a wide sheet of bark.

Kodo looked warily at the fat brown twig the small boy held out to him. His stomach growled like a bad-tempered lizard. Was he hungry enough to eat wood? He looked at the deer the hunters had killed. Could he wait until the feast?

The boy tossed the offering into his own mouth, chewed and rolled his eyes with delight. He rifled through the shiny brown pods until he selected a plump one and offered it to Kodo.

Kodo took it, breathed deeply and slipped it into his mouth. He closed his eyes and forced himself to chew. He swallowed. Encouraged, the boy held out the dish and Kodo took another.

'Not a twig,' he said. 'Tastes good.'

He passed one to Maia.

'What is it?'

'Juicy. Good. Try it.'

She held it on her palm. The ridged shape was familiar. She was aware of the boy watching her. It wouldn't do to refuse to eat what he offered. And she was hungry. She bit the case, chewed, felt juice spurt into her mouth. And realised she was eating a cooked cocoon.

Kodo was happily munching another. He saw her expression.

71

'What is it?'

She picked up another grub in its crisp shell and broke it open with her thumbnail. She could see the plump, cooked grub and the net of thin strands which it had spun into a cocoon. She tried to rub one free. It was glued tight.

'I think they're cocoons.'

She looked at the boy, held up the brown shell and attempted to smile.

'Moth cocoons.'

She quickly drew the outline of a moon-moth in the sand. The boy leaned over and added a round eye high on both wing shapes.

Maia drew a shaky breath. 'I think we're eating moon-moths,' she murmured.

She picked up another baked case. The shape was right, if a little smaller than the silk cocoons Tareth had guarded. Was it possible? Did the Kuma have a moth-garden?

She sketched another moth in the sand and then made squiggles to suggest the low-growing thorn bushes in the cliff-top moth-garden.

The boy drew a tall tree with drooping branches, covered with leaves.

Not Tareth's moon-moths then, thought Maia. They didn't live in trees. And the nomadic people would have no need of a garden. They would know where to find food everwhere in this barren place.

She felt a stab of disappointment. For a wild moment she had thought to find another source of silk for Tareth.

She had taken the last of the silk. It was safe, hidden in her back-sack, with the cocoons and eggs she had collected. She

72

must give Tareth what little there was left from the moth-garden and hope that it was enough.

She nibbled her lip. Each sun-sleep she checked the bundles. Each step across the Hidden she worried that the eggs would hatch. Feared that if she didn't carry them swiftly to the Sun Palace there would be no more moon-moths, no more silk for Tareth to weave. She must persuade Var to leave here soon.

The boy nudged her knee. He pointed to his tree and threaded his fingers together, flapping them to mimic wings.

Maia's heart leapt. The boy hadn't drawn leaves. It was a tree of moths. Close to the hunters' camp. Could they be like the moon-moths? Did the Sand People know what the moon-moths made?

There was so much of her has-been that she didn't know. Perhaps one of her family had found the moths and taken them from the Hidden to the Sun City. She loved the hot dry lands of the Hidden. Now she wondered if that was because her people had known and loved this land too. It was a difficult place, harsh and dangerous, but it called to her.

Maia swayed to the rhythm of the shuffling feet. The dancers leapt across the fire, throwing shadows of animals on to the rocks. The woman sitting beside her clapped to the beat, chanting a high bird call. Others joined in, passing the call from one to the next. Maia heard Var's voice.

She sat in a spiral of sound. The cries became urgent, the dancers parted, clashed their spears and throwing sticks. A huge bird leapt across the fire, spinning and whirling among the dancers. Maia held her breath as spears were raised, shaken at the bird, threatening to stab it. And then she saw that it wasn't a bird but a tall man, jangling bones and shells, his cloak of feathers turning him into a huge avian.

The man-bird strutted towards her, arms raised like wings. His face was a mask painted with bands of red and white, his eyes rimmed with black. He was a figure from a night-wake. He lunged forward. She tried not to flinch. The strings of shells on the gourds he carried rattled like the Watcher's stones as he shook them above her head.

The smell of grease and feathers and bitter leaves made her eyes water. The gourds rattled, feet stamped, the wings of his cloak hung over her and she felt as if she would suffocate. The dusty feathers brushed her head, the cloak whispered and he whirled away, back into the dancers who spun around him until all Maia could see was a swirl of arms, raised spears, sparks flying into the darkness, and above them all the huge hunter's moon. Var, his dark eyes gleaming, turned to her and leaned close.

'The hunt was good. Their shaman has welcomed you.'

Maia watched as the man-bird threw himself among the hunters. She shied away as the shaman flung up his wings and sank to the ground. Beside her Var cried out, his call echoed by the watchers round the fire.

The hunters moved back from the huddle of feathers and a line of figures drifted towards the fire. They circled the dead bird, raising and lowering their arms as if they were flying. They were like small birds flocking in the grasslands at the edge of the Hidden. The dances told the stories of the Kuma. Just as the story-coat told the tales of her family and Khandar.

Kodo gripped her hand. Maia glanced at him. He was staring at the shadows, not the dancers.

Maia looked and saw what he saw. The children were not birds.

The dark shapes fluttering across the rocks were moths.

CHAPTER TWELVE

Kodo opened his fist. The crushed silk whispered. He had gone to sleep holding it and had woken from strange night-wakes where figures spun through billowing smoke and chased him, spears held above their heads. He groaned. He had eaten too well. He could still taste the baked meats, the creamy flesh of tubers, the sweet ooze of plump grubs which popped when he bit into their crisp skin.

He sat up. All around him figures lay where they had fallen after the wild dancing. The moon had grown pale. It would be light soon. A finger of gold gilded the edge of a low line of hills. He hoped they marked the end of the harsh, dry land. He wanted to be rid of it. He hated how Maia loved watching the ever-changing play of shapes and colours as the sun rose and fell across rock and sand. He hated the grit which stung and chafed and lodged in every crease of skin and clothes. It was like walking endlessly across a hot, baked lizard scrape. At least the lizards had the sense to lay their eggs close to the cool sun-deeps.

The silk in his hand murmured again. It whispered of water lapping, of wind filling a sail, of leaves rattling on trees. Kodo wrapped the silk strand around his tattooed thumb and heard the sound of lizards waking in their pound. He could smell the smoke seeping through the reed roofs of the huts in the Stilt Village. His mother Jakarta would be waking to blow embers into flame to cook his grandfather's thick seed porridge. He felt a wave of longing to be there. The silk felt it too.

Kodo crept through the sleeping hunters, following the prompting of the silk. Several stirred as he passed. He waited until they were still and set off again.

At the edge of the fire circle he almost fell over a heap of feathers. The shaman's cloak. He stroked the silk and stole silently from the camp. He could return using his own tracks. Then a small hand grasped his. It was the boy who had fed him roasted grubs. He led Kodo behind a rock. Kodo put his fingers to his lips, chewed and gestured, making the fluttering movements of flying moths. The silk on his thumb sighed. The boy reached out to touch it.

Kodo pushed the silk inside his tunic out of sight, rubbed his stomach and chewed again.

The boy nodded and set off into the desert.

Nefrar twitched. His tail flicked across Maia's legs, waking her. She opened her eyes and stared up at the stars, still muzzy with sleep. Var lay flat on his back beside her, breathing softly, Tiki sitting upright on his chest.

As she sat up, the rat ran off. Maia felt for her back-sack. The cord was still knotted, the contents undisturbed.

She brushed sand from the bag and unfastened the cord, feeling inside, counting the small bundles. The leaf wrappings rustled under her fingers. They were dry, perhaps too dry. She tried to recall the instructions Tareth had given her about the best way to care for the cocoons and eggs. She would be glad to give him the bag and be free of the silk.

She was thirsty. She thought about the taste and warmth of chay. Her hands and toes were cold, even though she'd slept close to the heaps of ash and embers from the fire the hunters had built for the feast to celebrate a good hunt. They had eaten well. The food had made Kodo happy. She glanced at the sleeping cheetah and noticed the shallow hollow in the sand beside him. Kodo had gone.

Surely he knew better than to wander away from the fire and leave the safety of the camp? She nibbled her thumbnail, remembering how strange he had been as they watched the dancing. They had both recognised the moths. Kodo knew about moths and the moth-garden.

Suddenly she knew where Kodo was. He was trying to find the moth tree.

Without stopping to think, she crossed softly to his sleeping hollow. She could see footprints in the dust, leading away. She looked back. Nefrar still snored, his nose resting on her back-sack. Var hadn't stirred.

Maia followed the faint trail. She skirted the bundle of feathers, glad that the nomads too were sunk in exhausted sleep even though the first pale sun touched the dusty-winged cloak, fringing it with amber.

As she skirted the rock-face by the hunters' halt she saw a figure, sitting cross-legged facing the rising sun. It wasn't Kodo. He turned and she saw the painted black and white mask of the shaman. The paint was streaked with sweat but she could still recognise the face of the large horned deer the hunters had killed for the feast. And now she could see the animal's tail with its long whisk of black hair hitched to the shaman's belt.

The shaman rose. The shells on his ankles and belt chuckled as he moved. She wondered if he carried truth-telling stones.

'Sun's greetings, fire-bringer,' he said, tasting the words as if they were unfamiliar.

Maia's heart missed a beat. He knew what she was. He spoke her language.

She flicked her fingers.

'The sun's greeting, the wind's blessing and the earth's song be yours, truth seeker,' she answered.

The shaman's eyes narrowed. 'What does a Sun Catcher want with the Kuma? Why have you come here with one of our lost?'

Maia felt a frisson of shock. He saw it.

'The hunters told me that your eyes spat fire. They feared they would be burned by your anger, Sun Catcher.'

'I didn't harm them,' said Maia.

He nodded. 'They were not harmed. But why have you brought fire to the Kuma?'

'I haven't,' Maia denied. 'I didn't seek the Kuma. I didn't know that the sands held a secret people.'

'The Kuma do not choose to be found. Yet you are here, Sun Catcher.'

'On my way to the mountains where I must catch the sun again.'

'For what purpose? Do you bring danger? As did the rest of your kind, fire-bringer?'

She had a sudden memory of Elin. And the Wulf Kin. Had Elin waged war on the Kuma while Tareth hid her in the Cliff Village?

'No! Never.' She wasn't like Elin. She stood tall, her chin high. 'I am a Sun Catcher. Not a Death Bringer. I must catch the sun so that the cold of wolf-walk dies and the land can grow warm. So that the snows melt and new-leaf can begin. And so my people don't starve. Var, who you call 'lost', is my guide. And Kodo, the lizard boy, goes with us to the Sun City. We wish you no harm.'

He stepped towards her. The shells muttered.

'The stories of the Kuma tell another truth. Catchers are to be feared. They made this a dead land. Once it was a green place. There were many birds and beasts and full rivers. A land of plenty. The Sun People brought fire. And the land became as it is. And we who remained became the Kuma, people of the sand.'

He came closer. Maia stood her ground.

'Sun-catching brings life…'

'The land tells the story. The sand and the rocks cannot lie.'

'The Catcher brings light and warmth,' protested Maia.

She remembered how fragile the land had been when it was locked in the dark of wolf-walk, how Azbarak had said the city was close to starvation. Remembered the terrible power that she could summon.

She swallowed. 'I don't destroy.'

'Yet you bring danger and fire. And my people must hide.'

Maia shook her head. The eagle feather brushed her shoulder. 'No.'

He stared at her. 'Come,' he commanded. 'I will show you the has-been.' He spun away from her and set off along the rock-face.

Maia glanced back at the camp wishing she had brought Nefrar or Var. She didn't want to listen to the accusations of a magic man. She wanted to find Kodo.

'Come,' called the shaman. 'Or will you live with a lie in your heart when you can see what is true, fire-bringer?'

Maia clenched her fists. She was a Sun Catcher.

'Wait!' she answered. 'Show me.'

CHAPTER THIRTEEN

Maia squeezed between the rocks. She could hear water. A tree clung to a crack in the rock face. She could smell it as she passed. It smelled just like the bonesetter's cave above the weed beds. She touched the grey leaves and her finger felt numb. Perhaps it was a desert heal-leaf.

The gully opened out and she stood beside a pool. The rocks were stained red where water had leached from a tiny crevice. A few green plants with long thin leaves clustered around the water. She saw the flicker of a snake. The shaman stood on an outcrop. He beckoned. She scrambled up and crouched beside him and almost tumbled over in surprise.

The rock was covered with drawings. Etched into the stone she could see three long-necked creatures with tiny heads and patterned skin, a spindly horned deer, a snake, a winged bird with legs like the houses in Kodo's village, a herd of horses with stripes and running stick men with spears following them. She traced the shape of a small deer and found below it the outlines of several plump ground-feeding birds. The pictures continued across the rock face. She saw a flying water bird, a long-nosed lizard on its belly, more stick figures and a hand print, smaller than hers. She placed her palm against it.

'The has-been story,' said the shaman. 'Kuma hunters made this. To show the animals they knew before the sands came. Before the rivers became salt and dried. To show a green land.'

Maia thought of the way into the Hidden. Of the grasslands at the edge of the Vast which had become low scrub-covered hills, flat dusty riverbeds, stretches of sand and sharp stones and the waves of dunes too high to see over as they trudged through the valleys between them. There had been little sign of life. How could the rock story be right?

She glanced at him. He understood the question in her eyes.

He led the way round the bulge of carved rock, across wind-worn boulders to a wall of flat stone. Huge fissures ran across it. This rock had pictures too. Maia felt the hairs on the back of her neck prickle.

A battle raged across the surface of the stone. Archers, spearmen, stick figures with slingshots. Bodies trampled beneath them. Other figures struggling, locked together. A tall figure emerging from the flaming disc of a sun. Smaller ones with fire in their hands standing beside the sun disc. Figures curled on the ground, others running away. And above them all, rivers of fire running down the side of a hill.

The shaman pointed to the sun disc figure. 'Sun Catcher,' he said. 'Fire.'

Maia stood, trying to make sense of what she saw.

'The Kuma ran to the Hidden. They became the wind that blows the sand,' continued the shaman.

Maia studied the running figures. Did she see a battle, or an escape? Had fire destroyed them, not Sun Catcher fire, but fire cascading down on them from the hill?

'What happened . . . to them?' she gestured towards the fire carriers and the Catcher.

The shaman touched her arm. He showed her a smaller image. Of a tall, dying figure, clasping a long blade. The shaman shrugged. 'Fire,' he repeated. 'Death.'

Shaken, Maia turned away. It was a stone story, she told herself. A tale from the far has-been. The images were not of her family.

'I don't bring death,' she said and clambered across the boulders away from the rock pictures.

As she reached the small pool she saw Kodo. He was smiling, his eyes looked wide and dark and drugged.

'Come and see,' he said.

The path became a dead end. A tree with drooping branches grew close to the cliff-face. A tree with leaves that fluttered although the air between the rocks was still. Kodo crossed to the tree and sat beneath it. He held out his hand and a moth settled on it, its long tongue tasting the moisture on his fingers.

'It's all right,' said Kodo dreamily.

Maia sat beside him, staring up at the branches. The leaves were opening and closing. Not leaves, she realised: moths.

'What's all right?' she asked.

Kodo smiled at her. 'The silk was angry. When you set fire to the garden.'

Maia's heart bumped.

'You set the cliffs on fire,' said Kodo. He pulled a strip of silk from his tunic. The moth on his hand flew onto it. The silk sighed.

Maia leaned forward, brushed the moth aside and snatched the silk. 'Where did you get this?'

Kodo flinched and quick as a striking snake snapped the silk from her fingers and stuffed it inside his tunic.

'It's mine. The silk was angry with you,' he muttered. 'It sang to me.'

'You stole it!' accused Maia.

Kodo held his hand to his stomach as if he was afraid that she would tear his tunic and take the cloth from him.

'I took it from your back-sack,' he admitted.

'And you call Tiki a thief!'

'The silk called me,' Kodo explained fretfully. 'It always does. It was angry. But not anymore. It has found the moths. Everything's all right.'

Maia felt like shaking him. He spoke as if he were half asleep. Was he in a silk dream? She knelt in front of him, forcing him to look at her.

'The silk is Tareth's. Not yours. I'm taking it to Tareth.'

He frowned at her. 'I know you are. The Watcher said. It's in your back-sack.' He touched her shoulder. He tried to get up. 'Where's your bag?'

Maia pushed him back against the tree. 'Nefrar's guarding it.'

85

'That's good. He'll keep the rat away. Rats eat cocoons. And eggs. No more silk if he does that. You shouldn't let him near you.'

He was rambling. It must be the tree. Or the moths. Maia glared up at the branches and saw drops of dew on the branches. The resting insects were unfurling their long tongues and dripping them into the gleaming beads.

'Don't trust Var. You have to take the silk to Tareth. You have to go to the Sun City. You have to hurry.'

She pulled him to his feet. He protested and tried to wriggle free.

'We must get back,' she told him roughly. 'Come on.' She dragged him clear of the tree. 'I've left the bag with Nefrar and Var.'

'Don't trust him,' muttered Kodo. He shook his head as if to clear it. 'His rat's a thief. Shouldn't have left your bag with him. The cocoons aren't safe.'

They plunged through the gully, past the pool and out into the open. There was no sign of the shaman. The small boy was waiting for them.

He mimed a runner, then pointed back at the camp. He started trotting towards it.

Away from the tree, Kodo seemed to wake up.

'Why are you here?'

'Looking for you. You shouldn't wander off.'

'Nor should you,' retorted Kodo, hiding his pleasure that she had worried about him.

Kodo sprinted off. Maia chased him. When she reached the fire pit the Kuma were clustered together like buzzing bees round a honeycomb, bending over something on the ground. She saw Var standing with them. Caught a glimpse of the shaman with his painted face gesturing in the centre of the crowd. The buzz grew louder, angrier.

She skirted round them to her sleeping hollow. Her back-sack no longer lay in the sand.

And Nefrar had gone.

Chapter Fourteen

Maia fought her way through the excited crush.

'What have you done to him?' she screamed.

The crowd gave way beneath her furious onslaught. The shaman caught her arm as she crashed into a man, destroying the lines he was drawing on the sand. She was pushed aside. The hunters muttered angrily. She reeled, her mind full of fear and the images on the rock, of the beasts the nomads had hunted, killed. She shook her head to clear it. Nefrar was not by the fire. Had they harmed Yanna's cat?

'What have you done to him? Where's Nefrar?'

Hands grabbed her, hauled her to her feet, bundled her through the hissing hunters until she was standing outside the ring. She brushed them away and glared at Var. Kodo stood open-mouthed, staring at her as if she had lost all sense. Her anger boiled.

'Where's Nefrar?' she shouted at Var. 'And where's my back-sack?'

His bird bright eyes never leaving her face, Var slipped the cord from his shoulders and held out her bag.

'If your rat's stolen anything . . .' she growled. She snatched it from him. It was the shaman's fault with his rock stories. And Kodo's for silk-dreaming again. She ripped the bag open, feeling inside, counting the bundles. They were all there. She tugged the fastening tight and swung it onto her shoulder and felt the anger drain from her, leaving her weak.

She folded her arms round herself, hugging tight until the wild beat of her heart slowed. She forced herself to look at Var.

'Where is he?' she asked.

'Gone when I woke. I thought he was with you.'

'He was asleep by the fire.'

Kodo crouched beside her. 'He'll have gone hunting.'

'Why? He ate all he needed.'

'He'll be . . . exploring?'

'Without me?' She bit her lip. 'I thought the Kuma had killed him for his skin.' Her voice wobbled. She looked up at Var. 'I'm sorry for . . .' She bit her lip. 'I have offended the Kuma. They're angry.'

'Frightened,' said Var.

'Frightened? Of me?' Maia's heart sank. She had confirmed their beliefs about dangerous Catchers.

He glanced across at the cluster of men and women. As he did so the group broke up, started collecting spears and bundles. One extinguished the fire.

Maia followed his gaze. 'They're leaving,' she guessed.

89

'Because of what I am. A fire-bringer.'

Var shook his head. 'It's not you. They shared a feast. You're welcome among the Kuma.'

Maia gestured at the activity, 'Then why are they going to leave?'

'The Kuma go to hide. A runner brought word.'

Var looked at Maia. 'The stronghold at Altara is under attack,' he said. 'The runner heard that men who shine in the sun, wear wolf pelts and run with beasts larger than deer make war on the women.'

'Altara! The Wulf Kin have attacked the Warrior Women?' The ground seemed to shift under her feet. 'That's where Nefrar is. He's gone to find Yanna. To fight with her.' She remembered the big cat's disturbed sleep. He had paced round the firepit during the feast, too restless to sit for long. 'Was he gone before the runner came?' she asked Var.

Var nodded.

The cat had known Altara was in danger. Why hadn't she? Why hadn't the silk warned her?

'I must follow Nefrar. Go to Altara.'

She remembered the soft shuffling feet of the shaven headed girls who had stared at her as they filed past to the eating place and sleeping hall. Remembered their need to see the strange flame-haired visitor who brought hope. She thought of the women who had taught her to become an archer and a warrior. 'I must help the Warrior Women.'

Kodo grabbed her arm. 'You can't.'

She pulled herself free. 'I must. I owe them my life.'

'You have to take the silk to Tareth. To the Sun City. You can't go to Altara. You can't take the moth eggs into battle.

Not against the Wulf Kin. What if you are hurt? Captured? They will find the silk. You said Tareth needed you to return swiftly,' Kodo reminded her fiercely.

Maia clenched her fists. 'I cannot abandon Nefrar. I cannot leave Altara to its fate,' she said.

'You cannot endanger the silk.'

'But I must.'

The shaman approached. 'So battle comes, Catcher,' he said.

'Not of my making.'

The shaman looked at Var. 'You are welcome to come with us, lost one,' he said.

Maia heard Var's intake of breath and saw him glance at the sand-painted figures who were slipping in single file from the hunters' camp. She saw his eyes before they became blank again as he hid his thoughts. The shaman nodded as if Var had spoken.

The shaman turned to Kodo. 'If this struggle is not yours, you too may walk and hunt with us.'

Kodo shook his head. 'I promised to return to the Sun City and the sun-deeps.' He glanced at Maia and then again at the shaman. 'If you could show me the way.'

Maia felt as if he had struck her.

'Someone must return,' he said. 'Someone must take the cocoons to Tareth. If you cannot then I will do as I promised the Watcher and carry it for you.'

'Kodo!'

He shrugged. 'You are a better warrior. The Warrior Women need you. And Var carries enough knives to slay many Wulf Kin. And he can run like Nefrar. You will go faster without me. Take a hunter's running blades and find

91

the cat. Save Altara. Then come to the city. Trust me. I'll take your back-sack home for you. I'll keep the silk safe.'

Maia was drowning in a wave of doubt. Could she expect Kodo to take the burden of the silk? He was right. It was foolish to carry the precious eggs into battle. She had told Tareth that she trusted Kodo with her life. Now she must prove it and trust him with something more precious: Tareth's to-come.

Kodo smiled at her worried face. 'At least this way the rat will stay with you and can't steal the eggs.'

She couldn't return his grin.

'Stay with the Kuma. We'll return when Altara is safe and go on together. It may be dangerous for you to go alone.'

Kodo raised his eyebrows.

She blushed. 'I know you are brave . . . but . . .'

'If the Wulf Kin are attacking Altara then they won't be hunting in the grasslands. I know how to follow the signs. I'll find the way to the city. The silk will be safe with me.'

Maia bit her lip. She had no choice.

'You must be strong,' she told him. 'Tareth will die if he doesn't make a new garden and weave silk. You mustn't sit and listen to dreams. You must go swiftly.'

Kodo faced down her fears. 'I understand what I need to do.'

A hunter approached him. Kodo held out his hand. Maia slipped the back-sack from her shoulders and put it on Kodo's.

'I know,' she said.

She stepped back. Raised her hand to the sun and flicked her fingers.

'The sun's greetings, the wind's blessing and the earth's song be yours, ' she said. She kept her voice steady, her eyes dry. 'Go swiftly, lizard boy.'

'And you,' said Kodo. He leaned forward, breaking the formality of the parting to give her a quick, clumsy hug. 'Remember the Wulf Kin poison their blades. Be safe.'

Maia watched as he jogged from the camp at the heels of a tall, thin nomad.

Var returned with running blades. He knelt to tie them to Maia's feet, wrapping the bindings round her ankles.

'The cat will be swift,' he said.

Maia adjusted her balance. It would be easier when she moved. 'So will we.' She held on to him, flexing her knees, testing the spring of the running blades. She was as tall as Var, their eyes level.

'Thank you for coming with me.'

'The lizard boy was right. I carry many knives.' He guided her for a few paces until she hit her stride.

He felt inside his tunic, checked that Tiki was resting against his belt and prepared to run.

'Come,' he called. 'We have Wulf Kin to hunt.'

Chapter Fifteen

The Wulf Kin's beast grumbled with pleasure as Caspia sank her fingers into its fur. At least the wulfen was pleased with her. Caspia felt her jaw relax. She had gritted her teeth so hard to stop herself screaming at Elin that she'd heard her bones groan. She could not, would not, try to wear the story-coat again. She knew what it would be like. She'd feel helpless as it took her thought-stealing ability and remained silent. She wouldn't put on the coat. Not until she knew the Catcher was dead. Then the silk would have no one. Xania the Story Singer was no more. The silk wanted a new singer. She would wear it only when she lifted the sun-stone to catch the sun. Then it would whisper for her.

She was still shaking with rage. She knew what Elin had shouted wasn't true. She was ready to be Queen. She would prove it. And show Urteth that she was worthy to be his daughter. His silence had been worse than Elin's anger as he listened to her mother's demands that she try again to listen to the stories in the coat. She remembered the strands of doubt and disappointment she'd unravelled in his thoughts.

The wulfen nudged her, dribbling on her skirt. She pushed its head aside. She knew how to show her father that she could be strong. She rose and beckoned to the Wulf Kin who would do as she commanded.

'Vultek. Fetch my pony. And supplies.'

'Are we leaving, lady?'

'To find a Wulf Kin raiding party.'

His small eyes gleamed. 'And ride with them?'

His eagerness banished any qualms. His loyalty was a balm. Urteth would be proud of her when she found his scavenging Wulf Kin and led them when they raided the herder families crossing the plains. She would bring him horses. Her temper cooled as she imagined what she would tell her father when she returned to the Tower.

'Yes.'

They rode hard and fast, following Vultek's wulfen when it picked up a scent trail. Then they raced ahead until they smelled smoke and found a small band of Wulf Kin clustered round a camp fire.

Vultek grabbed Caspia's reins. 'I will ride first, lady, to see if they are Urteth's Wulf Kin.'

Caspia tugged her reins free. 'All Wulf Kin are loyal to Urteth.' She kneed her pony forward. 'And to me.' As she rode towards the group, she heard Vultek's knife scrape from its sheath and wondered if she was wise to go among them. Her father had summoned Wulf Kin from the teiga forests and far mountains. Perhaps these were strangers. Her thumb ring blazed red as she raised her hand.

'I come from Urteth,' she called.

A tall Wulf Kin separated from the pack. 'Greetings, Lady.'

He knew her. Caspia felt a tremor of relief. A wulfen circled her pony, sniffing. Caspia felt her mount go rigid and stroked its neck. She cast her thought-stealing net and caught curiosity, but no threat.

'Call off your wulfen. It's unsettling my horse.'

'You bring word?'

Caspia waited until the wulfen moved away. She swung from her horse. 'To join you.' She heard the murmur. 'To ride with you and find horses for my father. He needs many for the battle to come.' She strode to the fire. 'Have you seen herders?'

'Most have fled.'

'Then we must ride and search for them.' She crouched and took one of the sticks holding a joint of crisp-skinned lapran cooking above the embers. 'We've come far.' She gestured towards Vultek to untie the bag of supplies hanging from his saddle, 'And have food to share.' She took a bite of the meat. 'But none as tasty as this.'

She knew that she'd pushed the limits of hospitality by taking food before it was offered, but they were Wulf Kin and she was Caspia, daughter of Urteth and the Queen. They must accept her authority.

Vultek dropped the bag at the feet of the Wulf Kin. She noticed that he kept his hand on his knife hilt as he stood behind her. His wulfen panted at his side.

'Eat,' said the Wulf Kin slowly. 'And then we'll hunt.'

At a nod from their leader, the Wulf Kin round the fire shuffled to make room for Vultek to crouch beside Caspia. They watched him as he too snatched food from the embers. Then one of them tore open the small sack, tipped the contents on the ground and pushed the foodstuffs among his companions who started squabbling over the offerings.

They had been accepted.

Caspia smiled. 'Good.'

The herd of horses grazed below the rise where they halted. A child on a pony rode slowly round the edge of the herd. Close by was a nomad's yurt. Caspia felt a thrill of excitement. They had found a small family moving across the grasslands with their herds; an old man sitting by the tent watching a woman milking a hobbled mare and two children rolling in the grass.

'Round up the horses,' said Caspia. 'Urteth needs them. Follow.'

She urged her pony to trot.

The Wulf Kin yelled and raced past her. Their wulfen bounded, baying, towards the herd. Caspia heard the lone rider shout, saw him raise a stick as he tried to control the panic, heard the terrified squealing as the horses reared, tossing their heads, and fled from the wulfen.

The stampeding horses flattened the family yurt, tumbling the old man aside as he stood waving his arms and shouting, trampling him as they thundered past pursued by wulfen and yelling Wulf Kin. He didn't rise. This was not how it was meant to be. She was their leader. They should be following her. Caspia drummed her heels against her pony's flanks and careered after the Wulf Kin.

It was over before she had chance to draw breath. As she raced into the camp, a man staggered to his knees from the wreckage. Drawing his knife he charged. And was cut down like the tall grass scythed before leaf-fall to make fodder for beasts by Vultek's swinging blade. Caspia was almost unseated as her pony swerved to avoid the trampled tent. The woman who had been milking screamed at her children to run before she too lay lifeless, the pan of milk kicked over and spilling in the grass. Caspia gasped, seeing the bright flower of blood that bloomed at the woman's neck and stained her tunic. The children ran towards the long grass. Caspia tried to rein her pony. She thought she heard the wail of a baby. A small girl turned and ran back, arms reaching to grab the infant. And fell beneath the singing arc of the Wulf Kin blade which drank her life and the baby's too. Caspia felt a wave of nausea overwhelm her. She gagged. Swallowed and screamed at the Wulf Kin.

'Leave them! Leave them! Take the horses!'

Even if he heard her, it was too late. Vultek's wulfen had seen them.

'Vultek!' she screeched. 'No!'

She slipped from her pony and was sick. This was not how it was meant to be.

When it was over, Vultek found her crouching by her pony clinging to the reins as if to stop herself sinking into the earth. 'The young . . .' she gasped.

He cleaned his knife. 'It was swift. They would have died alone here.'

Caspia swallowed. She creaked to her feet. Straightened. And made herself look at him. She felt the warmth of the ring on her thumb as the sun touched the red stone and it glowed. It reminded her of what she was, *who* she was. He mustn't guess that she was horrified by the massacre.

'And the horses?' she demanded. A queen's daughter couldn't be weak.

'The Wulf Kin chase them. They will catch them and the boy who rode with them.'

She mounted stiffly. She didn't look at the body of the woman and her daughter.

'He is of no interest. It's the horses we want.' She gestured towards the disappearing herd and the pursuing Wulf Kin. 'Follow when you have buried them.'

And without glancing at the shattered camp, she rode away. She knew she would never forget this sight.

To prove that she was one of them she helped the Wulf Kin round up the herd. They were fine ponies, fat with grazing good grass during the warmth that had followed the sun-catch. Urteth would be pleased. There was no sign of the child who had guarded them. She cast her thought-stealing net wide, but caught no wimper of fear. She hoped he'd escaped. But he too could have fallen beneath pounding hooves.

She felt the buzz of pleasure which coloured the thoughts of the Wulf Kin. They showed no remorse. Neither should she. She told them to go ahead and take the ponies to Urteth. Then she rode on alone. The further she went from the scene of the raid, the cleaner the air seemed to become. Her mind cleared. And when Vultek joined her and she saw the chunk of lapis lazuli tied to his dagger sheath and knew he had robbed the bodies, she accepted the blue bead as a gift.

'For your first raid,' he said.

She hung it on her bridle. And thought how well it looked on her black pony. 'But not my last,' she said.

She stood in her stirrups and gazed across the empty grasslands. 'We should ride swiftly. Urteth will be anxious to hear what has happened.'

Wrapped in dreams of Urteth's pleasure, she didn't cast her thought-net. If she had, she might have found the faint echo of another traveller hurrying across the Vast.

Kodo tucked the two sticks into the back-sack, carefully avoiding the leaf-wrapped bundles. Each sun-sleep since the hunter guide and his family had departed he had used them to line up the stars as Var had shown him. He was sure that he was still following the right track.

He studied the sky hoping to see the clouds which often billowed above unseen mountains. Then he would know that the Sun City was close. But the sky was empty except for one small puff hanging in the distance above the grasslands. Perhaps there was water there.

He hitched the back-sack on his shoulder and checked the position of the sun and his shadow. Good. He could walk that way and, if there was water beneath the cloud, he would refill his leather pouch. As he set off, a water bird flew over. A good sign, thought Kodo, and lengthened his stride. He would use the catch-net he had made with the nomads. His mouth watered at the thought of the baked fowl he would cook at dusk.

That was the one thing Var had been good at: hunting. Kodo missed eating the food Var had found. Thinking of Var made him worry about Maia. He told himself that Nefrar and Var would watch over her. He wondered again if he should have stayed. Maia had always stood by him and he had let her go into danger without him.

He tried to squash his anxiety. It was not good to be alone with his thoughts. It had been easier when he had followed the nomad and his family who had shown him the way. The small boy who had fed him grubs had kept him cheerful. The mother had kept him busy foraging. The silent hunter had made them journey quickly until they reached the edge of this plain. Kodo knew that the man was anxious to rejoin the other nomads, but it had been a shock to wake a handful of sun-sleeps ago to find that they had vanished and he was alone.

He'd felt bereft even though he had been expecting it. They wouldn't leave their tribe and safety to take him all the way to the Sun City. He'd been comforted by the gifts of food they had left with a snare to catch small ground feeders. He had caught a lapran. Sitting by his small fire watching the fat spit into the flames and seeing a shower of shooting stars, he'd known that he could survive here, alone. What tales he would have to tell Maia.

He'd thought that the sun-deeps would carry him to the Sun City. But it was not to be. It would take him too far from his path. His fate was not to sail with Trader. Kodo put that regret aside. He might feel safer on the sun-deeps than he did here, but if Maia had crossed these plains to reach the Sun City, so could he.

His anxiety deepened with the thought of her decision to abandon the silk and fight. He broke into a jog, hoping the jolting gait would break his thoughts. It did. Lengthening his strides, watching where he placed his feet in the rough grass, he ran towards the wisp of cloud.

Caspia plucked the heads from the white flowers and threaded them into the grass circlet she had plaited. She placed the crown on her head and wandered to the edge of the wallow. Avoiding the mud churned by a herd of ponies which Vultek said had drunk there at sun-wake, she stared down at her reflection. Her face frowned back at her. She knew she had been foolish to give in to anger when she and Elin had argued.

Caspia squeezed her eyes shut, and tried to banish the memory of children running. She'd never forget the small girl who had fallen beneath Vultek's blade. She could taste bile. She swallowed and thought instead about the wild ride to catch the ponies. They were fine animals. Urteth would be pleased when the Wulf Kin drove them into the valley towards the Tower.

She glanced at her black pony. It stood, head down, up to its knees in water. It was lame. It had thrown her when it stumbled. She'd been careless, riding swiftly in her haste to reach Urteth. When Vultek returned with another mount for her he would feed the pony to his wulfen. She would insist that he killed it first, that he didn't send it fleeing across the Vast in terror pursued by his baying beast. She would spare the animal that. To leave it alone here would be cruel. It would be taken by wolves.

She watched a waterfowl scud from the grasses at the edge of the shallow pool, noting where it had been hiding. Perhaps it was sitting on a late clutch of eggs. Another bird joined it. Spit-cooked fowl would make a change from the dried strips of meat, shrivelled fruit and nuts, which was all she had eaten since leaving the Tower of Eagles. She would tell Vultek to catch them.

She turned away and gazed across the rolling grasslands, searching the Vast for movement. No one. She threw her thought-stealing net wide. Silence. She frowned. Since she'd worn the sun-helmet her thought-stealing gift was weak.

It was good to be alone. She had become tired of Vultek, his smell, his bold eyes, his presence at her side. Even his vicious wulfen had lost its appeal. She wished she had chosen another Wulf Kin to accompany her. But Vultek was loyal and useful and obeyed her. He had ridden to find her another pony when she had refused to ride behind him and insisted she must have her own mount. She had told him she would take his and make him ride his wulfen. She smiled, remembering his silent anger. But he had obeyed as she'd known he would.

Then she heard it. A whisper, no more. A thread from her thought-stealing net. She listened. But the air was empty, the only sound the faint sigh of the moving grass, a splash as the waterfowl took off in alarm. It flew past her, calling. Its mate joined it. She watched them circle several times, her pony flung up its head as they skimmed across her to land again, sending ripples across the surface. As the water grew still she heard the murmur again. Silk.

There was a movement. A figure. Too tiny to be Vultek returning with another pony. She flung her thoughts again but misjudged the cast. It was too far away for her. No thoughts, but something. And she had felt it before. She strode towards it.

The grass beneath her collapsed. She fell. She heard the crack as she tumbled through sticks. She hit the ground and screamed as her wrist snapped.

Kodo heard screaming. He stopped and fell to the ground. Cautiously raising his head, he peered over the grasses, turning slowly until he had searched all around his hiding place. The plains were empty. He pressed his ear to the ground listening for the thud of feet or hooves. Nothing.

He could see taller grasses ahead. He heard the cry of a

bird. Probably the waterfowl he had seen. The grass must hide a pool. He'd been so busy watching where he placed his feet as he ran that he hadn't realised how close it was.

He could see flicking ears and the head of a black pony. The ears twitched his way.

Kodo pulled his knife from its sheath and stole towards the twitching ears. He almost tumbled into a pit gaping at his feet. Crawling forwards he peered over. It was a hunter's trap: deep, the sides edged with sharpened sticks, some sheered off where something had fallen in.

He could just make out a pale face and hair the colour of flames.

'You!' said Caspia.

CHAPTER SIXTEEN

Even with her blue dress torn, her skin scratched and her face white with pain from her broken wrist, Caspia was still pretty. She could have been Maia's sister. Kodo knew he was staring and looked at his hands as he snapped one of his way-finder sticks. He tore a strip of fabric from his tunic. It wasn't clean. He ripped it into narrow bands.

'This will hurt,' he said. 'I must bind it, keep it straight.'

Caspia winced as he felt her wrist, easing the bone into line, but she didn't make a sound.

Kodo placed her arm on the stick.

'It needs healer's knit-bone,' he said.

He pulled his silk from his tunic, laying it across the break. Silk had helped his arm to heal when he had fallen in the moth-garden. It would help the bone to knit cleanly.

Caspia gasped. 'You found silk.' She touched it. 'I knew

you would.'

The silk shivered. Before he could change his mind and snatch back his gift, Kodo wrapped the torn tunic bands around the stick and over the silk to hold it tight against her arm. He heard the silk sigh as he hid it under the bindings.

'Yes,' he muttered as he tied a neat knot. He undid his water pouch from his belt and offered it to her. Her nose wrinkled as she tasted the water, but she smiled as she returned the bag.

'Thank you.'

Kodo blushed.

Caspia held up her bound arm, her hand clasping her wrist, trying to feel for the silk.

'I would have died if you hadn't come.'

'I was on my way to the Sun City. I heard you shout.'

Caspia's eyes widened. 'I'm going there too. We can go together. My horse is lame. She's resting. I was looking for heal-leaf for her when I fell.' She touched the long scratch on her face and neck, pulling her red hair forward to hide the mark. Fire glinted in the heart of the stone on the thumb ring she wore. Tiny white flowers from her grass crown fell from her hair into her lap. She pulled off the woven band. 'I go to speak with the new Queen. I have failed her. I have no silk to give her.' She picked up the flowers and let them tumble like a shower of falling stars. 'She will be angry.'

'No.' Kodo watched the drift of flowers.

'Do you go alone?'

Kodo nodded.

'Then let me come with you,' said Caspia. 'I'm afraid to stay here alone with a lame pony.' She held up her bound arm. 'We will be safer together.'

Kodo got to his feet. 'We can lead the pony. There may be heal-leaf close by. I've healed lizards. I can help your mare.'

He splashed across the wallow and led the pony to the edge of the water, watching its gait carefully. He felt its legs. 'There's no swelling. No heat. The cold of the water will have helped. If I lead her, perhaps you can ride.'

He glanced at Caspia. Her face was pale.

'Perhaps,' she murmured.

'You should rest,' he added, 'while I search for heal-leaf.'

Caspia twisted awkwardly, trying to fluff the grass into a nest with her sound hand.

Kodo helped her, found her padded felt saddle and placed it in the hollow. She lay against it and winced, holding her arm.

'This will help.' Kodo picked up Maia's discarded back-sack, removed the Kuma hunter's bird net and snare and the unbroken way-finder stick, then tucked the bag beside her to support her wrist.

Caspia closed her eyes. 'I knew you would help me. I'm glad you found me.'

Kodo gazed down at her. She was hurt and needed him in a way Maia never had. He wondered what had happened to Caspia's tiny colour-changing lizards. Perhaps they'd run off and were swimming in the wallow.

He glanced at the sun, judged the length of his shadow and patted her pony. It would be best to let them both rest here. He would catch a waterfowl, build a fire, sleep. And continue to the city with them at sun-wake.

Caspia opened her eyes as he moved away. She watched

him set a snare and gather leaves. She shifted her arm so it lay more comfortably on his bag. It was lumpy. It rustled. She wondered what was kept in there. She felt for the fastenings. And let her hand fall away as Kodo glanced back. She would discover his secret soon enough. Her arm hurt. She would sleep. Then she would steal his thoughts, become his friend, make him loyal to her, not the Sun Catcher. She would wait for Vultek's return. She would take the silk. Lead the lizard boy to the Tower of Eagles, away from the Sun City. Let the Catcher learn what she, Caspia, had done. If she hadn't mistaken the drift of the lizard boy's thoughts, the theft of the silk and his capture would bring the Catcher to find him. And she and Urteth and the eagles would be waiting for her.

She lay listening for the return of Vultek. He would come soon. She smiled at the thought of Kodo's surprise. She heard the startled squawk of a bird. The boy was a skilled hunter. Vultek wouldn't go hungry when he returned. She wondered if the boy was right and her pony was barely lame. She was glad. The black pony was swift and beautiful and she had taught it to run freely beside a wulfen and not to sweat and quiver or try to bolt whenever the Wulf Kin's beasts were near.

Caspia touched the binding on her wrist. She was sure she could feel the silk. It was silent, but she knew it listened.

She slept.

109

The smell woke him. Leather, grease, fur, sweat.

Kodo tried to jerk upright. The weight on his chest prevented him. A sharp point pricked his neck.

'Don't harm him,' Caspia's voice was sleepy.

The knee on his chest moved, pressed harder. Leather creaked.

He turned his head towards her voice, straining to see in the dark.

'Caspia?'

The skin of his neck split as the knife shifted. Warm blood oozed.

'Lie still, lizard-lover, or I'll slit your throat and feed you to the beast.' Fetid breath carried the snarl. Kodo felt a surge of nausea.

Something large moved in the dark behind his head. Kodo's hair stood on end. Saliva dropped onto his face, into his eyes and his mouth. He gagged, almost choked as terror and memory merged in a flashback and he bit back a scream.

Wulfen. A vicious bear-wolf. A beast on the cliff springing at him. Crushing gaping jaws missing him by a hair's breadth. The raking claws knocking him flat, lacerating his skin. Screaming. Maia throwing fire. Killing the beast. Saving him. Burning him.

Kodo shuddered. Wulfen ran with the Wulf Kin.

Through the slime he could see the glimmer of the embers, the glint of red hair, the flash of her ring as Caspia threw a stick onto the fire. His way-finder stick, he thought wildly. How could he plot his way to the Sun City?

She leaned over him. 'A pity you woke,' she said. 'Don't be afraid.'

'Are you a prisoner?' croaked Kodo. 'Has he harmed you?'

'No. He wouldn't dare. I am the Queen's daughter.'

Kodo nodded. The knife bit again.

'Don't harm him,' said Caspia sharply.

The knife moved away. Kodo breathed deeply. Good. At least the Wulf Kin listened to her.

He sat up and felt the beast's hot breath on his neck.

Caspia touched his arm. 'We'll have to go with him. He'll take us to the Tower of Eagles.'

Confused, Kodo whispered: 'Not the Sun City?' He glanced towards the fire where the Wulf Kin was crouching. Maia's back-sack lay in Caspia's sleep hollow.

'No,' said Caspia. 'Wulf Kin are no longer welcome in the city. He has two ponies. We can ride together.'

'Will the black pony follow?'

Caspia nodded.

'Good,' muttered Kodo. 'Then we can escape. When he sleeps. Ride to the city.'

'With the silk?' breathed Caspia.

'Yes.'

He felt for his knife. The sheath was empty.

'Do you have a knife?' he asked urgently.

'In my belt.'

'Hide it,' urged Kodo. He looked across at the Wulf Kin. The man stared back at him. He snarled and bared his pointed teeth. The Wulf Kin lowered his face and chewed the fur on the back of his hand. He was like his beast, thought Kodo.

'I need my back-sack. Say it's yours. He seems to listen to you.'

'He is frightened of my father,' said Caspia. 'I will try to persuade him not to bind you. Say that you are a poor rider and will fall, delay him if he ties you.'

'Good idea,' muttered Kodo.

The Wulf Kin was looking at them suspiciously. He rose to his feet. 'What are you saying?' he demanded.

Caspia rose to her feet. 'He bleeds. You've cut him.'

'I should have cut his throat.'

'He will ride with me,' said Caspia. She held up her arm. 'I cannot ride alone with this.'

The Wulf Kin scowled.

Caspia moved back to her sleep hollow. She put her head in her hands. 'I'm hurt. I can't ride through the dark. I will fall. If I'm injured my father will punish you when he finds you. And I promise he will hear what you have done.'

She glared at the Wulf Kin. 'I will not stir until sun-wake. You will do well to remember what I am. *Who* I am.'

The Wulf Kin nodded slowly. 'Sleep while you can. We ride at sun-wake. The beast will watch.' He glowered at Kodo. 'Try to escape and he will tear you limb from limb.'

Caspia lay down. She gave Kodo a tiny smile. He felt the soft probe of her thoughts. Her excitement.

Despite his fear, Kodo felt his heart leap too. Caspia was bold and resourceful. Together they would trick the Wulf Kin and escape.

CHAPTER SEVENTEEN

Smoke hung in the sky, climbing high enough to blot out the sinking sun. The fire must be huge. She was too late. Maia quickened her pace.

Var caught her hand, forcing her to go faster until she felt as if she was flying like a hunting eagle. They breasted a rise and Var skidded to a halt, knocking her down and falling beside her.

'Keep down,' he panted.

She could feel thudding. Her heart pounded madly against her ribs. Then she realised that the drumming came from the ground.

'Riders,' said Var. 'Coming fast. This way.'

She could hear shouts. She raised her head and had her face shoved into the grass as Var pushed her down. 'Stay still.'

What he asked was impossible. The thud of flying hooves

was closer, the yells louder. They would be trampled. She tensed, ready to spring. She heard the song of an arrow as it hummed overhead and shuddered into the grass. Var rolled onto her, shielding her with his body.

A pair of horses sped past, leaping over them. Its rider yelled, released an arrow. Maia heard the thrum of the bowstring, the wild silk song as it spun on the bow. Warrior Women.

Var surged to his feet, knives in his hands. He spun on his running blades, watching the horses. Maia sat up and saw a rider guiding her careering pony in a tight circle with her knees as she pulled another arrow from her thigh quiver. Var drew back his right hand.

'No!' shrieked Maia.

He teetered on the tips of his blades.

'Altara. Warriors!' shouted Maia. She scrambled to her feet, lost her balance on her blades and crashed to the ground. An arrow zipped over her.

Var yelled. He took several running strides and leapt, pulling the warrior from her mount. They rolled, locked together. The pony whirled, reared, balancing on its hind legs, poised to smash down on Var once its fallen archer had struggled clear.

'Friends!' screamed Maia. 'Altara! Friends!'

'Catcher?' A muffled question came from the grass.

Maia saw Var pushed aside. He slithered away from the striking horse hooves. A woman with long, dark, plaited hair sat up.

'Catcher?'

From the corner of her eye she glimpsed Var rise from the grass and grab the rearing pony's reins. He was safe. Beyond him a second rider wheeled and rode back towards them. Reassured that it was a Warrior, she turned to the woman in the grass.

'Yanna?'

A long, lean, dappled shape flowed past the sitting archer and knocked Maia flying. She felt as if the skin was being stripped from her face as she was washed by a rough tongue. Paws with sharp claws kneaded her rib cage. Breath whooshed from her lungs as the cat collapsed on her.

'Nefrar!'

She hugged him. She heard his rumble of greeting and breathed again as he tumbled off her and paced over to Var to nudge him in the back as he gentled Yanna's pony.

She was pulled upright and almost swung off her feet by the strength of Yanna's hug.

The mounted warrior reached them. 'The Wulf Kin are gone, Yanna.' She glanced over her shoulder, 'We should ride to Altara before they realise we are alone here and attack again. They are many.'

Yanna stooped to pick up her fallen bow. 'They've fled for a reason. Perhaps to tempt us into the open while more of their kind launch another attack.' She grabbed the reins from Var and vaulted into the saddle. She looked down at him and frowned. She glanced at Maia who was pulling off her running blades and held out her hand so that Maia could swing up behind her.

'I thought you had suddenly grown tall, Catcher,' she laughed.

Maia hung on to her waist. Nefrar was already streaking towards the smoke with Var racing beside him. At least Var

wouldn't have to wait for her to keep up, she thought, as
Yanna sent her pony galloping after them.

Tareth sat hunched, head bowed, beside a line of bodies.
A grey-robed healer, her face smeared with dirt and blood,
moved along the line. Behind her limped a bald girl carrying
a bowl and rags for binding wounds. Maia saw the healer
stop beside Tareth, his eagle feather brushing his shoulder.
The healer moved on. He wasn't hurt. Maia felt a rush of
relief as she slid from Yanna's pony and ran to him.

She flung herself onto her knees. His tunic was torn and
singed, his face blackened with smoke, an angry red mark
scored his cheek. She touched it with the tip of her finger.

'You need heal-leaf,' she said.

Tareth hugged her. 'It's nothing. Others have more need.'
He held her away from him, examining her face. 'How are
you here?' He looked past her. 'I feared the worst when
Yanna's cheetah came without you.' He pulled her closer, his
arms tight around her. She could feel his heart thud against
her, its beat uneven. She smelled the smoke in his clothes.

'Is Altara . . . destroyed?'

Tareth coughed. 'We've quenched the flames, but Altara
is no more. And many warriors are injured and dead. Have
you brought help?'

Maia shook her head. 'Just myself and another. We heard
that Altara was attacked. So we followed Nefrar. We saw the

smoke and found Yanna pursuing Wulf Kin.' She held his hand, still not believing that he was here, safe, alive. 'Found you.'

'Has Razek returned with you? Or Kodo?'

Maia shook her head. 'The weed beds need their Storm Chaser. Kodo is on his way to the Sun City. He will reach it soon.' She crossed her thumbs. A gesture Tareth noticed.

He rubbed his smoke-reddened eyes. 'Kodo left you?' he demanded in disbelief.

Maia sat back on her heels. 'He didn't leave me alone. Nefrar and Var were with me.'

She'd seen Var removing his running blades as he waited beside Nefrar. Yanna hovered close, flipping the braid on her bow, obviously anxious to hear what Maia had to say, yet unwilling to intrude on the reunion of the Weaver and his daughter.

Maia beckoned. Yanna placed her hand on Var's back, shoving him forward.

'This is Var,' Maia said.

Tareth looked up at him. Then he reached for his knife, pushing Maia aside.

'You!' he exclaimed.

As fast as a spitting cobra Yanna's blade was in her hand. She pressed it against the base of Var's spine. 'I knew I'd seen your face.' Her arm snaked round his throat, jerking his head back.

Var tensed. Yanna kneed him viciously in the back of the knees.

'Be still!'

Var watched Tareth as he reached for his crutch and hauled himself to his feet.

'How did you escape?' demanded Tareth.

Yanna tightened her grip. 'Who freed you?' she snarled.

Maia looked from one to the other in disbelief.

'Escape?' she demanded.

Var's glance flickered to Maia. He said nothing.

'He's my guide,' protested Maia. 'The Watcher sent him from the cliffs to take us across the Vast.'

'Guide? Him? He followed you from the Sun City to the weed beds?'

'I was sent,' said Var. 'I protect.'

'Protect!' snarled Yanna. 'You tried to knife Tareth in the palace. I saw you myself. You came to kill him and the Sun Catcher.'

Tareth's eyes narrowed. 'Who do you protect?'

'Me,' said Maia. 'He protects me. The Watcher told me.'

'He's a killer,' said Tareth. 'Who set you free? Who sent you from the city?'

Var was silent.

'He protected us, kept us alive,' insisted Maia. 'He came to find me when the Marsh Lord imprisoned me in his holdfast.' She saw their disbelief. 'The Watcher sent him. Nefrar likes him.' She looked at Var. 'Tell them!'

'Nefrar,' echoed Yanna. Her grip loosened. 'The cat is usually choosy about his friends.'

Var twisted free but made no attempt to defend himself.

'Tell them who sent you,' repeated Maia. 'Tell them about the Watcher's stones.'

Var shrugged. Watching the tip of Yanna's blade he slipped his left hand into his tunic. He opened it. On his palm lay a smooth, white stone.

Maia took it. The runes scratched on the surface seem to wriggle. 'The Watcher gave him the stone,' she said, holding it out to Tareth.

He barely glanced at it. 'The Watcher didn't send you from Khandar,' he accused Var. 'Who did? Why are you here?'

Tiki chose that moment to squirm from the neck of Var's tunic. He climbed on to his shoulder, whiskers twitching, his small, bright eyes on Yanna.

A look of distaste crossed Yanna's face.

Var turned to Tareth.

'Azbarak the Keeper sent me. He helped me escape from the locked room. He sent me to follow the Catcher and her companions.'

'Azbarak?' gasped Maia and Tareth.

'He sent you and your rat to find and kill the Catcher,' claimed Yanna. 'Azbarak is Elin's creature.'

CHAPTER EIGHTEEN

'Azbarak serves the Sun City and the Queen. What is he to you?' asked Tareth.

Var hated questions. Questions needed lies to answer them if he was to be safe.

'Nefrar would not be mistaken.' Maia commented. 'I don't believe you wish me harm.'

She turned to Tareth. 'Kodo and I would have died without Var's help.'

Tareth grunted in disbelief.

'I trust him. I trust the Watcher and her stones. Whatever was in the has-been. Whatever he has been.'

She looked at Var. 'You've shown me nothing but friendship since we left the Watcher's cairn. My father says that Azbarak the Keeper supports the Queen. But which queen? Is Azbarak loyal to me or does he still serve Elin?'

Var decided not to tell all of the truth. The has-been was a secret place. He didn't invite anyone there. Yet he had led this girl across the Vast. He had watched her come to love the desert almost as much as he did.

'I owe you and the cat Nefrar my life,' he said. 'You pulled me from the sun-deeps when I should have drowned in the storm.'

He was surprised at the intensity of Tareth's dark gaze.

'You owe Maia your life, so you cannot kill her,' said Tareth.

Var nodded. 'But I owe Azbarak my life too.'

'Azbarak?' Maia was incredulous. 'The fat Keeper?'

'He finds,' said Var slowly.

'Finds?'

'He found me lost, wandering, with no family or tribe. I could not survive alone in the desert. I was young. Many children are found. They live in the holdfast in his village. It's a good place. And he teaches us because we have no tribe to show us what to do. We are trained in many things.'

'He trains children to kill?' Tareth was horrified.

'He teaches us to survive,' said Var. He thought of the skills he and the other children learned. Skills that enabled them to live by their wits. 'I was an acrobat, a juggler.' A thief too, he thought, as well as a tracker, a runner and a spy. And a killer. 'I learned to fight.'

'A band of warrior urchins,' said Yanna. 'Azbarak is filling the Sun Palace with such an army.'

'I was summoned to the city,' Var continued. 'I was told to protect, to follow the Sun Catcher.'

He didn't tell them that Elin, the red witch, had summoned him too.

'The Keeper knew that the Catcher's way was long and dangerous and feared that her companions wouldn't keep her safe. He said to me, "what do a lizard boy and a weed boy know?"' Var's scorn for Kodo and Razek's fighting skills coloured his voice. 'Azbarak didn't know that the cat would go with her. I was saved from the storm. The old woman and her birds helped me. They told me I must help the Catcher. We set off to the Sun City. We crossed the Vast together with the lizard boy and the cat. The Kuma found us and spoke of battle. The lizard boy continues to the city with a guide from the Kuma. I came here with the Catcher to help defend Altara.'

He looked at Tareth. 'I did not harm her.'

Tareth shook his head as if to clear his thoughts.

'Is this true?' he asked Maia.

'What he says is true,' she said carefully. She didn't say that she wondered how much of his story he had left unsaid. Var was a boy of silence and shadows. And secrets.

She glanced at Nefrar and was reassured. Nefrar was a good judge. 'I've always trusted Var. I still do. And so did the Watcher's stones.'

Tareth returned his knife to its sheath. 'Then I thank you for what you've done to protect Maia when I could not,' he told Var.

Var could read nothing in the dark-haired man's face. Instead he asked, 'Are the Wulf Kin defeated?'

'They try to weaken us, now that the Warrior Women are without the protection of the stronghold. But the archers are strong, although we are few. And their hunting cats fight the wulfen.'

As if to prove his words Maia heard the thunder of hooves, the high, fierce song of the warriors as a band of archers galloped past and raced towards a mounted group advancing across the plain. A shower of arrows fell among the attackers. Maia saw the Wulf Kin scatter with the Warriors chasing them. Once again the pursuit was brief as the women and their cheetahs slowed their breakneck charge and released a last flight of arrows after the retreating enemy.

Attack, retreat, rally, attack. The Wulf Kin seemed to be trying to exhaust the Warriors and their supply of arrows. Were they waiting for reinforcements too? Yanna's warriors were well trained. They could hold the Wulf Kin for as long as their arrows lasted. And they were ferocious hand-to-hand fighters.

If I were a Wulf Kin, thought Maia, I would wait until sun-sleep and slip into the Warriors' camp under cover of darkness, not mount attacks in the open. She glanced at Yanna.

'They are playing with us,' said Yanna grimly. 'Keeping us here to defend the injured. We need to take them to the Sun City.'

'They'll be safe there,' said Tareth. 'Wulf Kin won't attack the Sun City.'

Yet the Wulf Kin had decided to attack the Warrior Women's stronghold, thought Maia. Had Elin sent them? Elin had promised to punish the Warriors for turning against her and supporting Maia. She looked at the wounded and the smoking remains of Yanna's stronghold. This was her revenge. Altara was burning as she had said it would.

The healer approached with heal-leaf. She made Tareth

sit, ignored his protest and slathered his cheek with green salve. A young Warrior, so newly trained that her hair was short and spiky like fledged feathers, offered Maia a stale flatbread from the bundle she carried. Maia looked round.

'Is KiKya with you?' she asked. 'Has her wing healed?'

'She can fly,' said Tareth. 'She is here.'

Maia breathed a sigh of relief.

'The silk helped the healing. And now you have come we will make a moth-garden.' He took a flatbread. He lowered his voice so that only she could hear. 'Did you bring all of the old silk with the cocoons and eggs?' He saw the look on Maia's face. 'Did you wrap the eggs well? Keep them cool?' His voice was urgent. 'Where are they Maia?'

He looked for her back-sack, and realised that she wasn't wearing one. That only curved running blades hung from the strap slung across her shoulder.

'Where is the silk?'

Maia found it hard to meet his eyes. 'Safe.' She crossed her thumbs behind her back where he couldn't see. 'I didn't dare bring the silk into danger. Into battle. Kodo has the silk. He's taking to the Palace.'

'You gave it to Kodo? Knowing that Kodo can hear it sing? That he'll never be free of it. That it's dangerous for him to listen to the silk?'

'Yes,' said Maia. 'Kodo is strong.'

CHAPTER NINETEEN

K odo gripped the lead rope with one hand and tried not to hold Caspia too tightly with the other.

The Wulf Kin, riding alongside, glowered. He hadn't been pleased when Caspia had insisted that her black pony should not be left behind. Nor when she'd said that she would ride with Kodo so that she didn't fall from the jittery pony the Wulf Kin had brought. It was terrified of the wulfen, tossing its head, its eyes rolling as it tried to rear. Yet Caspia was able to control it with one hand.

She was amazing, thought Kodo. Even the Wulf Kin was in awe of her. Caspia's bravery made him strong. If the wild ride hadn't stolen his breath he would have laughed aloud.

Beneath the back-sack he could feel the knife sheath nestling between his shoulder blades. The Wulf Kin had only taken his belt knife. Kodo was glad Maia had insisted he take her shoulder knife when they'd parted.

He risked a glance over his shoulder. The black pony was moving well. The heal-leaf had helped. They would need two ponies when he and Caspia escaped.

The Wulf Kin shouted, pointed upwards. 'The eagles are coming.'

Three eagles flew overhead. Kodo could hear them calling. His heart leapt. A single Wulf Kin and his beast would be no match for three Eagle Hunters and their birds.

One bird seemed to stall in the sky, then dropped lower, swooping over them, spooking Caspia's pony. It swerved. Kodo saw a flash of golden eyes, felt the beat of wings as the eagle swept past, so close that its black wingtips almost touched him. He saw its trailing jesses.

He heard Caspia laugh as the bird climbed fast and was attacked by the two other eagles. They tumbled, shrieking, towards the riders. The wulfen bayed and bounded towards them.

The Wulf Kin punched his fist in the air, grinning as his beast chased after them. Kodo felt sick. He couldn't believe what he had just seen.

Caspia reined in her pony. She sat listening. The Wulf Kin rode close. Kodo dropped the lead rein. He lifted his hand as if to scratch his neck. This was the moment. He felt for Maia's knife.

A pain stabbed behind his eyes. He felt as if he was drowning.

'Wait.' He heard the soft voice clearly, but he knew that no one had spoken out loud. He tried to grasp the hilt of Maia's knife and couldn't feel it. His hand, his mind were numb. 'Not yet,' said the voice in his head.

It was a relief to drop his hand. He felt pinpricks fizz along his fingers as if he had trapped them beneath a rock. The pain in his head stopped.

'Someone comes,' said Caspia.

A group of mounted Wulf Kin cantered towards them. One held an eagle on his wrist.

Caspia turned in the saddle. Her eyes were very blue as she whispered. 'Do nothing. It's no use. They are too many.'

A tall man with a black wolfskin over his shoulders raised his hand. Kodo swallowed as he saw the man's face. It was badly scarred.

'Did you see the eagles?' called Urteth.

Kodo grabbed Caspia's waist to stop himself tumbling from the pony. He knew that voice.

'Yes, father,' said Caspia.

Urteth rode closer. 'Greetings, Caspia.'

Kodo felt the man's gaze. It was like ice. He tried not to shudder.

'So, what have you found, daughter?'

'Silk,' said Caspia. 'The boy carries silk.'

Maia crouched beside Yanna as she fletched new arrows and examined the puncture mark on Nefrar's shoulder. It had healed well. She lifted his paw. The pads were worn but uninjured. She rubbed his fur the wrong way. Nefrar

127

rumbled with pleasure.

'He knew you needed him,' she told Yanna. 'He left me to find you.'

Yanna's hands didn't pause as she deftly inserted a flight feather into a notch on an arrow shaft, but her eyes were bright.

'Nefrar and I have hunted together since he was a kit still suckling his mother's milk. We are old friends.' She tickled the cat with the flint tip of her arrow.

Nefrar yawned and batted the arrow away

'He was restless under the horned moon,' Maia said. 'He woke suddenly during sun-sleep. I thought we were going to be attacked, but there was nothing in the darkness.'

Yanna dropped the twine she was using. She stared at the cat.

'Not me,' she said slowly. 'Another.' She picked up a second arrow. 'Our youngest warrior, Bekta, fell in the mountains on her way to warn the Sun City. The Warriors feared an attack. Her cheetah also died. Perhaps Nefrar felt his passing.' She paused, her head bowed, looking at, but not seeing, her idle hands. She gave a start and reached for her twist of twine.

'Bekta had tied her message to her cheetah thinking the cat would reach us. A hunter found it. Tareth and I left for Altara with the Warriors who had remained with me in the Sun City. We were too few to prevent the Wulf Kin setting fire to the holdfast, but we drove them off. They attack us still. But we will have our revenge. And when we have rid the plains of them and their foul wulfen, we will rebuild our stronghold.'

She looked at Maia, seeing the trouble on her face. 'Tareth has spent many sun-wakes watching for your return. KiKya, his new eagle, did not take your place in his heart.'

'We parted in coldness. I injured the eagle because I didn't listen,' confessed Maia. 'And I've disappointed him with the choices I've made. I should have taken the silk to the Sun Palace, not left it with Kodo. I haven't brought Tareth the silk he needs, nor found a new Story Singer. I have failed him.'

Yanna shook her head. 'You are the Sun Catcher. The choices will always be hard.'

Maia watched Tareth offering scraps of meat to KiKya who perched on his abandoned saddle. She wondered if the eagle would fly into a rage if she approached her.

She found Var standing beside her. He stooped to rub Nefrar's head.

'Come and meet Tareth's eagle,' she said, glad to have company.

Var's eyes were wary.

'Her name is KiKya. She hates me!'

He fell into step beside her, 'Why?'

'A Sun Catcher cannot fly eagles.' She shrugged away her hurt. 'I thought I could. I injured her when I went to the mountains and took her from her eyrie.'

'It would be good to have an eagle,' said Var. 'To see with an eagle's eyes. To have far sight.'

'Yes,' sighed Maia. It was also good that Var seemed to understand. 'That was my dream before the Watcher found my destiny in her stones.'

Var wondered if he imagined the chill of the two pebbles that rested against his skin. The Watcher's strange gift held an unwelcome fascination. When he was alone before sleep, he held them, listened for a sign. But there was nothing. He should throw them away, he thought. And knew that he wouldn't.

Var flicked his fingers in greeting as they reached Tareth and his young eagle. The bird glared at him. He knew the eagle showed the thoughts her master hid. The bird was fierce, angry, dangerous. He sent a silent command to his rat to stay where he was.

'I have come to say farewell,' he said, and realised that perhaps this was the choice the Watcher knew he must make. To break his promises. To leave the Catcher in the safekeeping of her friends rather than take her to Azbarak in the Sun City. He didn't know what Azbarak would do. He'd seen him change his allegiance. Var knew that if he went to the city his choice would be between his loyalty to the Keeper and to Maia. That might be the choice between the black stone and the white. He didn't want to choose. Leaving was easier.

He saw light flare in Tareth's dark eyes and looked at Maia. 'You no longer need my help to reach the city, Sun Catcher. Nor my other skills.' He managed a half smile, remembering her quick hands tossing her throwing knives. She could almost match him and he was the best of Azbarak's assassins. 'You are quick and deadly. And there are many here to take my place. I must return.' But perhaps not to Azbarak, or his stronghold in the foothills. He felt his heart lift as he thought of sands and silences.

Maia felt as if the breath had been thumped from her lungs.

'You can't leave,' she said. 'It's dangerous. There are Wulf

Kin. Their wulfen will track you.'

She realised how foolish she sounded. If Var didn't wish to be seen, he would vanish like the sleep-fogs of the desert melting before the sun.

'We need you.' She swallowed her pride. 'I need you.'

Var shook his head. 'You have many warriors. One less will make little difference.'

She knew he was wrong.

'When this is over,' she gestured to the smoke and blackened timbers that were all that remained of Yanna's stronghold. 'When Altara is avenged I will return to the desert and find the Kuma. I need to understand the images on the rocks.'

She looked at Tareth, the man she called father. 'I saw a Sun Catcher drawn on the rocks. A battle. Strange beasts. Stories of the has-been. Stories which made the shaman afraid. I need to know what they mean. The Kuma believe Sun Catchers brought war and destroyed their land.' She clenched her fists. 'Is that my to-come? To be a Death Bringer, like my sister Elin? Is that another secret you kept from me?'

Tareth winced.

Maia felt a beat of remorse. He had tried to protect her, to tell her only what he thought she must know. But, she'd made so many mistakes. She knew the stories on the rock were important.

She turned to Var. 'The Kuma are secret, hidden, unseen. Even the story-coat doesn't whisper their name. I'll never find them. The shaman named you the lost one. He knew that you were from the sands. If you are with us, then the Kuma will let me find them. The shaman will take us to the rock paintings. Tareth may know what they mean.'

Var hesitated.

'Stay. Come with us,' said Maia. 'With Tareth and KiKya and me. Help us fight.'

CHAPTER TWENTY

Four eagles skimmed across the smoking ruins, flying low and fast, their wingtips almost brushing the grass. Maia ducked as one of the birds separated from the others and powered towards her, talons outstretched. She heard Tareth cry out and saw KiKya leap onto his fist.

Off-balance, she flung out her arm in an attempt to ward off the incoming bird. Wings beating frantically, its talons gripped her arm. Fierce yellow eyes glared at her. The eagle folded its wings to perch on her wrist. And stayed there.

Its companions swooped above Tareth, circled and flew back to the riders careering towards the Warrior Women's camp.

Staring bemused at the bird on her forearm, Maia thought she heard the high singing call of Eagle Hunters. But all her attention was on the golden eagle. Why didn't her sun-fire burn the bird as it had burned the fledgling, KiKya? The eagle shifted, shook its tail feathers and settled more comfortably on her arm. Its talons were as sharp as flint arrowheads. Maia winced as they dug into her flesh and wished she was wearing a gauntlet. It would protect the bird when it felt her fire. She tensed and waited for it to plunge from her arm. The eagle sat still.

She looked around. Var pulled off his belt. Tiki squeaked as he tumbled to the ground and was hit by two falling stones. He saw the eagle on Maia's wrist and raced for the shelter of Tareth's saddlebags as Var wrapped the leather belt round Maia's fist. She breathed a sigh of relief as the bird stepped onto the leather strap.

But why did it sit there? How was it possible?

'Sun Catcher. We meet again. I see Garha remembers you.'

A man in a padded coat swung from his sweating pony and strode towards her. He dropped to one knee.

'Greetings Catcher.' He rose grinning at her. 'The eagles brought news. We have come to fight with you and the archers and then to escort you to the Sun City,' he said, as he had done when he had ridden to find her at the Crystal Cave. 'You are needed there. They say that the red witch has gathered an army at the Tower of Eagles and will ride to the Sun Palace.'

'Egon,' said Maia with delight and touched her forehead to greet him. 'You are welcome.'

The eagle on her fist bobbed. She felt the tip of his beak tap against her cheek before it stepped onto the stocky Eagle Hunter's gauntlet. Maia blinked. To hide the upsurge of emotion, she looked past Egon to where the other riders were dismounting.

'Does Huan ride with you?'

'My son follows,' said Egon. He flicked his fingers at Tareth, his expression suddenly serious. 'Sun's greetings, Weaver. We met with a band of Wulf Kin and their beasts. Our eagles fought well. The wulfen were no match for them. Neither they nor their Wulf Kin will attack Altara again.' He nodded to Yanna as she joined them. 'We came when the Warrior Women summoned us, although there are also many threats in the mountains.' He put his hand in his waist pouch, drew out a lump of meat and fed it to Garha.

'Wulf Kin raiding parties ride into the valleys to attack villages. The nomads find their animals slaughtered. Hunters have been killed. The passes are unsafe. Urteth has summoned many Wulf Kin. They are leaving the forests and their mountain caves. They go to join him at the Tower. Eagles fight eagles.'

Maia felt a flicker of fear. Then told herself she was being foolish. Kodo wouldn't pass near these bands of Wulf Kin on his way to the Sun City.

Tareth frowned. 'Eagles fighting?'

Egon's eyes were bleak. 'My son has seen them.' He stroked Garha's breast and fed her another scrap. 'I sent him to the Tower. I didn't believe the rumours. But I trust him. Urteth is capturing eagles. They are flying with their wulfen.'

Maia stared at the pinpricks of light that surrounded them. She counted them. Three. Yanna had told her that Wulf Kin encircled them. The unlit fire must be the camp of the Wulf Kin that Egon and the Eagle Hunters had killed.

She returned to their hearth, and threw another branch onto the blaze. The flames leapt and cast shadows across the faces of her companions.

'We should use the darkness,' she said. 'Attack while they sleep.'

'At sun-wake,' said Yanna. 'I will send the archers into their camps.'

'The eagles will fight with you,' said Egon.

'We must attack together,' added Tareth. 'And leave some warriors here to protect the injured.'

'And weaken our attack,' said Maia.

'We cannot leave the healers to defend the hurt,' snapped Tareth.

'There are three fires. Three bands to fight.'

Maia turned to Var. He sat hugging his knees beyond the flickering light. She saw Tiki's shadow on his shoulder.

She hesitated. 'Can you kill the Wulf Kin in the dark?'

'I am a Death Bringer,' said Var. He scooped up his rat and tucked him in his tunic as he rose to his feet. 'Keep the fire burning bright. They'll be watching. Walk in front of the flames, so that they can see that you are here. Sharpen your weapons. Let the wounded cry out. Keep watch and give the watchers a burning torch. The Wulf Kin should see a camp preparing to sleep.'

'I'm coming with you,' said Maia. She checked her knives and remembered she had given her shoulder blade to Kodo.

'No!' said Tareth.

Egon rose to his feet. 'I will go.'

'It's better if I go alone.'

'I will ride with you.'

Var frowned. 'Can you move without a sound? Can you kill silently?'

'I am a hunter. And you cannot go alone into their camp,' Egon said

Var looked as if he was going to argue. Then he shrugged. 'You will need to blacken your face and hands. Take twine. A throwing knife. Your eagle stays.'

Maia wonderd why Egon should be chosen to go with Var and not her. Her hand fell to her knife. She would insist that she shared the danger.

Var glanced at her. 'This is a matter of darkness not light. It is not for you, Sun Catcher.' His gaze flickered to Egon. 'It will be easier if I go alone.'

Egon turned to the fire, pulled a fragment of charred log from the ashes. He crouched, spat on his fingers and touched the log and winced as the heat scorched his skin. He looked at Tareth. 'A throwing knife?'

Tareth slowly pulled a knife from his shoulder sheath. 'The wulfen will be awake,' he said. 'They will scent you even if they cannot hear or see you and raise the alarm. You will never reach the fires. We will ride and attack at sun-wake.'

Egon held out his hand. 'There will be fewer if the boy and I succeed. I will leave Garha to fly with you.'

Reluctantly Tareth passed him his knife.

Egon slipped it through his belt. Yanna silently searched

for twine in her belt pouch.

'An archer should go with you,' she said. She turned to speak to Var. 'I will send . . .' Her voice faded. 'Where . . .?'

Var had disappeared.

'He only knows how to fight alone,' said Maia. 'In the silence and shadows.'

Maia walked round the fire, stepping over the long bundle lying with its feet almost in the ashes. Yanna stirred and sat up.

'Has he returned?'

Tareth rubbed his eyes. 'No.'

Egon grunted and added more fuel to the flames then took Maia's place to patrol backwards and forwards.

Maia stamped her feet and blew on her fingers to warm them as she searched the darkness. She closed her eyes, straining to hear. One of the wounded cried out, she heard the healer's voice, a pony moved restlessly, the fire crackled. She tried to block out the sounds of the camp. Beyond the firelight, the darkness was dense and silent. The stars seemed very bright. She looked for the seven sister stars, turning slowly until she saw them low on the horizon.

The hairs on the back of her neck stood on end as a wulfen howled.

CHAPTER TWENTY-ONE

The wulfen slobbered. A rope of saliva swung from its jaws and dripped onto Kodo's arm. He tried not to flinch.

He still had night-wakes when he relived the wulfen attack above the bee cave when Maia had saved him. She had flamed the beast, pulled down the rays of the sun and melted it with fire. He swallowed the acid taste in his mouth and wished that Maia was here.

He drew his knee to his chest, making himself smaller, aching from the chill of the stone floor. The warmth from the huge fire didn't reach his corner of the great hall. Wulf Kin sprawled near the heat, close to their beasts. Kodo wished this wulfen would move to the fire too. He could hear its rumbling breath, smell its foul, drenching drool. The tall, gaunt Wulf Kin who had shoved him into the solar sat in the shadows watching him. He was old, the fur on his arms was grizzled, flecked with grey. But he was strong.

Kodo had felt his wiry power as he had dragged him from the pony and dumped him. The old Wulf Kin had been the one to lift Caspia from the saddle. He had led her almost protectively into the tower. Kodo had seen the other Wulf Kin make way for him as Urteth waited on the steps. Old Grey-Fur was important.

The man-beast looked at him as if wondering what a lizard boy was doing there. Why he wasn't a prisoner. He opened his mouth to pick his teeth. Kodo saw his sharp-filed incisors and shivered.

'What does the Lady Caspia want with a shaking boy?' grunted the Wulf Kin. 'You will be poor sport for my wulfen.' He poked Kodo's thigh. 'Too little meat on your bones. But perhaps you will run fast, boy, when the wulfen hunt you.'

Kodo's nails dug into his palms. He wouldn't let the Wulf Kin see him tremble. He summoned up the image of the giant lizards, of Doon and Toon. The red-crests would be able crush the wolf-bear with a single snap of their jaws. They were fierce and powerful and he was their rider. He drew strength from the thought.

'Caspia is my friend,' he managed to say although his mouth was as dry as the sands where the Kuma hunted.

'Friend!' mocked the Wulf Kin. 'Then why are you left here with me?' He nodded beyond the fire where Kodo could see Caspia talking to a seated woman. Kodo's eyes widened as he recognised Elin, the red witch. 'Why are you not welcomed by them?'

'I will be,' he muttered as much to reassure himself as to

answer the taunts of the Wulf Kin. 'I saved Caspia's life.'

Zartev's hard eyes glinted. 'Then I will give you a head start when I set my wulfen on you.'

Kodo reached up to scratch his neck. The blood drained from his face as he felt the empty sheath. Maia had given him the knife. It had been Tareth's gift to her. He shouldn't have listened to Caspia and let her take it from him. But she'd told him that he had no need of knives because he was with her. She said she would tell her father what he had done and Urteth would welcome him, reward him. Her voice had been sweet, her words convincing. He'd been dazzled by her.

He shook his head in an attempt to remember what Caspia had said and done. What he'd witnessed on the wild ride to the stone tower. He'd been stunned by the sudden appearance of Urteth and his Wulf Kin. Shocked by the sight of eagles battling. Afraid. He felt a creeping sense of desperation and guilt that he had been taken without a struggle.

His thoughts drifted like strands of weed on the keep nets. His head felt full of fog. And through the fog a finger curled, probing, listening. Was it the silk? Kodo flinched. The touch was cold. He felt the tug of the straps of Maia's back-sack. He had to keep the cocoons safe. They were the last remnants of the moths from the cliffs. Maia had trusted him with them.

He had to keep them safe.

Elin watched impatiently as the old healer unbound the torn strips wrapped round Caspia's wrist.

'Foolish beyond belief to fall from a pony,' she said. 'How will you ride at the head of the Wulf Kin?'

'I can ride.'

'With an eagle?' demanded Elin. 'You must look like a queen. How could you be so careless?'

'It was a wolf pit,' said Caspia sullenly. 'The boy pulled me out. I thought you would be glad.'

'Better to have flung him in the pit than to bring him here,' said Urteth. 'He's no use to us.'

'Then send him into the mountains and let the Wulf Kin have him,' said Elin. 'They grow bored. Let the eagles fly with their wulfen to hunt him.'

'He has silk,' Caspia winced. The healer was not as gentle as Kodo had been. She pushed the woman aside and peeled the silk strand from her hand. 'He gave me this.' She held it up. It was so thin that she could see the outlines of her mother's face through it.

Elin leaned forward to twitch it from her. Hesitated and brushed her fingers swiftly across it. 'Old silk,' she said scornfully. 'Weathered. Torn. Useless.'

'He has more,' said Caspia.

Elin's eyes narrowed. 'Where did he find it?'

'He didn't say,' said Caspia.

'Have all of your skills deserted you, daughter?' Elin's voice was sharp. 'Since when can't you steal his thoughts?'

Since the sun-helmet stole mine and plunged me into darkness and the story-coat didn't sing, thought Caspia. Since then thought-stealing was no longer easy. She touched

142

the tattered silk strip and mind-searched for Kodo. She couldn't find him.

Caspia closed her eyes and scrunched the silk in her hand. And found a tangle of confused images of large lizards and wulfen shot through with red streaks of fear. Then a jolt of disbelief and images of eagles. She felt her name. Probed deeper and lost the connection as he blocked her. She frowned.

'He was the Sun Catcher's companion,' she said. 'She will have given him the silk.'

'Where would she find old silk?' demanded Elin. 'There was none in the palace. The Weaver was desperate for it. Will be desperate still. He no longer has the story-coat and its memories. He needs silk, even if it's old.'

'Silk which Caspia says the boy has found,' said Urteth. 'And was taking to the Sun Palace,' he guessed. He looked at his daughter.

'Does he trust you?'

Caspia smiled. 'Yes.'

'Good. Make him tell you where he found the silk. And find out if there's more. Take what silk he has. Discover where the Sun Catcher is.'

Caspia nodded.

Urteth glanced at Elin. 'The boy may be useful after all. If the attack on Altara didn't tempt Tareth to leave the Sun Palace, he will come to us now. He wants the silk. The Eagle Hunters who skulk in the hills, watching us, will tell him that the boy rode here with Caspia. The boy's capture plays into our hands. Tareth will leave the city to rescue him. We will finally meet at the Tower of Eagles where we played as boys.'

Elin's eyes gleamed. 'A meeting I would like to see,' she said.

143

Urteth shook his head. 'You will ride to the Sun Palace with Caspia as we planned. She must claim the sun-stone. Azbarak will support you, help you overthrow the Sun Catcher. Altara has been destroyed as you wished. The archers cannot help the city. And I will deal with my treacherous brother Tareth and join you before the sun-catch.'

'And the Sun Catcher?' asked Caspia.

'She is mine,' said Elin. 'The last of my sisters who tries to take what is mine by right, who dares to steal the throne, will sing with the voices of our lost sisters in the story-coat.'

Kodo fidgeted under Urteth's brooding gaze hoping that the man in the wolf-pelt wouldn't remember him. He hoped in vain.

Urteth frowned. 'I have seen you,' he said and glanced at the old Wulf Kin who had prodded Kodo across the sun hall.

'The boat at Haddra,' grunted Zartev. 'Traders.'

Kodo's shoulders sagged.

'You are a long way from the far-deeps, boy. What brings you across the grasslands to the Tower of Eagles?'

'The old one is right,' Kodo bluffed. 'My trades are with the . . . Horse People. My master wants rugs, turquoise, their golden horse carvings, horse hair.'

'Horse hair?'

'For the Marsh Lords, who live close to the sun-deeps, to wear on their bronze helmets,' said Kodo. 'For dyeing and weaving into strong cloth,' he added, only realising as the words left his tongue that he had said more than he should, remembering how they had smuggled the weaver, Tareth, from Trader's boat when Urteth and his Wulf Kin had been searching for Maia.

He stared over Urteth's shoulder at the curling carving on his chair, afraid to meet the man's eyes in case his panic showed. The black pelt across Urteth's shoulders bristled with life as the man leaned back in the chair, rubbing his hand guard.

'And wolf-pelts,' he croaked. 'The People of the Running Horses trap the wolves that stalk their horses and sheep. They trade the skins. Trader always needs wolf pelts.'

'And silk?'

'Not silk. Horse hair,' said Kodo. 'My master doesn't trade in silk. Rugs, beads, copper ingots, pots, sometimes the carved horns of huge fish, amber, turquoise and blue lapis lazuli when he can.'

'No silk?'

Kodo shook his head. He tried not to think about the back-sack and its precious cargo of cocoons and eggs. They hadn't ripped it from him. There was still a chance that Caspia had kept her promise. He swallowed. He mustn't think about the bag or the moths.

Urteth held out his hand. A band of silk was threaded round his fingers. Kodo forced himself to stand still. His hands shook with his need to snatch the cloth from Urteth.

'Yet you gave this to my daughter, not rugs or turquoise to match her eyes,' Urteth's voice was like the silk. Soft, smooth, dangerous.

'Oh that! Old scraps,' muttered Kodo 'For healing. Bought in a market. I gave it to her to heal her arm, broken when she fell into the pit. A trader needs healing-cloth to bind his injuries. It's soft. It comforts. I thought it would help Caspia until she found a healer with knit-bone.'

He noticed a softening of Urteth's expression. He decided to appeal to a father's affection.

'I placed her arm on a stick as my people's healer taught me and bound her wrist and gave her my scrap of healing cloth. Then I tended her pony who was lame and waited for the Wulf Kin to come with another horse.'

He drew a deep breath and smiled. 'And she doesn't need my chips of turquoise. Her pony already wears the blue good-fortune bead that the horse women hang from their ears.'

He heard the Wulf Kin grunt. Urteth was amused.

'You like my daughter?'

Kodo nodded.

'Yet you lied and told her you had found silk.' Urteth's words spat at him like the venom of a striking cobra, almost numbing his thoughts with fear.

'I– I . . . wanted to please her,' he stuttered. 'Not admit that I had so little . . . Only . . . A bit . . . From an old woman in a market. And a few cocoons.'

'Cocoons?'

'Good to eat, roasted on a pan.' He shrugged off Maia's back-sack and scrabbled inside, finding a bundle, tearing the leaves from it, fumbling with the strand of silk wrapping the cocoons, pushing it deep into the sack and pulling out a handful of cocoons. His hand trembled. 'Trader cooks them,

146

eats them and pounds some to dust to mix with his chay when the fogs of the far-deeps chill his bones and he coughs like a horse eating dusty fodder.'

Urteth leaned forwards and took a cocoon, rolling it between his thumb and forefinger. 'Good to eat?'

Kodo nodded. 'Baked brown. Crisp. Juicy inside,' he said honestly. 'Good to eat if you like maggots and spend your life in the far-deeps as Trader does.'

Urteth looked at him suspiciously. 'You have a tongue like silk.'

Kodo closed one hand round the cocoons, spread the fingers of the other wide. 'I'm a trader,' he said. 'I tell the story of the things I barter. Any cocoons I find I keep in my back-sack for my master. There are never enough.'

'So Trader, where are your rugs and your horse hair and your turquoise?'

Kodo tossed the cocoons into the back-sack, pulled the cord tight and slung the bag across his shoulders.

'Left safely with the Horse People while I searched for sky stones.' He hoped that like him Urteth had seen the shower of stars in the sky. 'I saw the falling lights, but there were no sky stones. I was on my way back to wait for the nomads and their pack animals and ride with them to find my master at Haddra. I found an injured girl instead.'

Urteth frowned at him. 'That much is true,' he said. 'You did help my daughter. As for the rest of your story . . .' he scowled and beckoned to the old Wulf Kin. 'Take him and his maggots away. Keep him safe. Elin will question him. Caspia wishes to speak to him, too.'

Kodo didn't feel the Wulf Kin grab his arm and push him

from the solar. He clutched the straps of Maia's back-sack as he was shoved hard in the back and tumbled through a dark doorway. He lay shivering, sweat running down his scalp, into his eyes as if he had a fever. His teeth chattered. He relived each heartbeat of Urteth's inquisition.

Kodo rolled onto his knees, pulled off the back-sack.

Caspia was coming. She wanted the silk. She would confuse him. Trick him. Steal his thoughts.

He had to hide it.

CHAPTER TWENTY-TWO

Maia placed her hand on the pony's nose to keep it silent. Egon was doing the same. He had already stripped the dangling gold animals from his bridle so that they didn't jingle as they rode towards the sunrise. His eagle Garha perched on the felt saddle waiting to step onto Egon's wrist. Yanna was adjusting the quiver strapped to her thigh. Maia could hear the whisper of the braids hanging from the archers' bows as they mounted their ponies and prepared to attack the last of the Wulf Kin camps that surrounded them.

She stroked her pony's neck, wishing it was Fionn who would carry her into the attack, but her copper-coloured horse, a gift from the Eagle Hunters, was still at the Sun City.

She glanced at Tareth. He was sitting on a pony, KiKya on his wrist, his twisted leg supported in the loops of leather he had fastened to his saddle so that he could ride and fight with them. The silver tip of his bow gleamed in the decorated quiver slung from his belt and strapped to his thigh. He wouldn't stay with the injured. She'd bitten back her objection when she had heard his decision to ride with Yanna and her archers. Of course he would ride against the Wulf Kin, his young eagle flying above him. In the cliff caves he had taught her to fight. He was a Warrior Weaver and Eagle Hunter. She felt a surge of pride replacing her anxiety. As if he caught her thoughts he looked at her. His smile was fierce as if his blood already sang with the joy of battle.

She lifted her fist to salute him and his fledgling eagle and muttered an invocation to keep both of them safe as she vaulted into her saddle. Egon's pony fell into step beside hers as they rode away from the ruin of Altara. She was glad she was riding with him. Glad to be fighting under the shrieking attack of Garha.

Her sun-fire had not harmed Garha. Egon had suggested that she could fly older, stronger eagles. That when Maia had stolen KiKya from her nest the little one was too young to resist a Catcher's fire. Especially as the Sun Catcher was young too and had not learned to fully control her strength.

Maia's spirits rose. There would be problems. But it was enough to know that she didn't harm all eagles. She urged her pony into a canter. She would believe Egon. She could be the Sun Catcher and hunt with eagles.

She heard the song of the Warrior Women's bow braids as Yanna's band of archers swung away from her to ride towards the farthest Wulf Kin camp. Tareth rode at their head. She watched him lift his arm, launch his eagle. She saw the light from the rising sun gild KiKya's wingtip as she circled, gaining height above him.

Egon was singing. His pony lengthened its stride. Garha shrieked and flew from the hunter's fist. Maia's pony struggled to keep pace. Half blinded by its flying mane as she crouched low over its neck, Maia saw a figure standing in the path of the careering Eagle Hunters.

Var. She yelled. He turned, ran, and then she was upon him. She saw him check, raise his hand, spring as her pony swept past. And somehow he caught her outstretched arm, flipped like a tumbler at a Gather and landed behind her. Before she could check her pony he was clinging on to her. She heard his breathless laugh. Felt him sway as an eagle swept low over them.

And among the yelling, singing band of Eagle Hunters she rode pell-mell into the Wulf Kin camp.

Chaos. Shouting. Wulfen baying. Screams.

Maia loosed an arrow as a dark shape leapt across the fire. Swayed, throwing up her arm to deflect a swinging knife thrust as she rode down a tall Wulf Kin. It thudded onto her arm guard. She felt the leather split. Felt the singing arc of Var's knife as he slashed at the Wulf Kin. Heard the bubbling cry, the clash of blade on bronze as the figure staggered. Her pony stormed across the fire, scattering burning embers, charging into a world of black and red. Confusion, heat and ringing blades.

A wulfen sprang, its jaws snapping a hair's breadth from her thigh. She swiped at it with her knife and lost her grip on the blade as it struck. Her pony staggered as the beast fell, its claws raking the saddlecloth, and was trampled beneath its hooves. Maia was flung onto the pony's neck. Var grabbed her tunic and yanked her back into the saddle before she tumbled.

The high, singing 'He! He!' warning of the archers riding on each side of her rang in her ears as they released their arrows at bounding wulfen.

Wheeling horses. Struggling figures. Clashing blades.

She charged at a Wulf Kin who was dragging a pony to its knees. Its rider fell. The Wulf Kin raised his blade as the Eagle Hunter rolled away. Maia tugged her knife from her boot. Before she could throw it, Var's knife hummed past her cheek. It struck the Wulf Kin's mail, the blade piercing the gleaming links. She saw the Wulf Kin reel. Then they were on him. He was knocked aside as her pony struck him. As he fell he caught her boot, trying to pull her from the horse. Maia lurched, kicked and he lost his grip as they swept past.

A huge, black beast lunged at her pony. The pony screamed. Maia leaned forward, lashed out with her knife and felt it sink into fur and flesh. Wrenched it free to stab again. Hot blood spurted across her hand.

Var flipped from the pony and landed on the beast. Maia saw his arm rise and fall. Maia lunged and stabbed again, felt her blade jar against bone. The wulfen fell, taking Var with it. Her mount wheeled away, throwing up its head in panic as a shrieking eagle plummeted, diving at the wulfen.

She heard Egon bellow. Saw the beast jack-knife, trying

to catch the eagle. Glimpsed Var clinging to the beast, then slipping beneath its belly. She tumbled from her frenzied pony, and hurled herself at the wulfen in a bid to save the eagle. She must help Var. No time for fire. No time for thought. She grabbed a fistful of fur. Raised her knife. Felt the beast tense. Felt its power.

The burly figure of Egon crashed into the wulfen, knocking her aside. The creature staggered, collapsed, crushing Var beneath it. Boy, beast and Eagle Hunter rolled together. The eagle shrieked and latched its talons over the wulfen's muzzle. Var rose shakily to his knees. Knives in both hands, he launched himself once more at the writhing wulfen. Blows, grunts. The stabbing bird was shaken off. The beast reared, fell back, and lay still.

Egon sat up, crawled to his grounded eagle. Var lay staring at the sky. Maia picked herself up. Fallen Wulf Kin and their beasts lay around the camp. Exhausted archers and Eagle Hunters moved among them, examined their own hurts, collected spent arrows, solemnly greeting each other as they met.

'Var?'

He raised his hand.

She swallowed with relief and turned to find her pony. It stood quivering, its reins held by an Eagle Hunter whose fox-fur hat had been knocked askew and whose cheek was bleeding. Scratch marks from the wulfen's claws scored the pony's neck. Maia examined them. They were not deep. Not fatal. Var's leap and the eagle's attack had saved it. She patted the pony. It snorted as it smelled the gore on her hands then nuzzled her shoulder.

'It is over, Catcher,' the Eagle Hunter passed her the reins, straightened his hat and wiped his cheek.

'Over,' agreed Egon, settling his eagle on his wrist. 'They couldn't withstand our fury. We have rid the plains of their evil. Those left at Altara are safe.'

Maia turned to search the grasslands. The last of the Wulf Kin fires was out. Tareth and Yanna must have overwhelmed the encampment they had attacked.

'The healers can take the injured to the Sun City where they will be cared for,' added Egon. 'It will be safe for them to cross the plains.'

Safe until Urteth hears of this, thought Maia.

She quailed at the thought of Elin and Urteth's vengeance. She would not say it aloud, but she feared that the burning of Altara was only the beginning of Elin's attempt to regain power. She would have no choice. Her story was etched on the rocks in the desert. It was the fate of the Sun Catcher to destroy. She must kill her sister.

Tareth studied the drawing Maia had made. She had scratched the images she had seen on the rocks in the ashes from the fire. Stick men with spears, overlooked by a tall figure wearing a sun disc and surrounded by archers. She had scored the ground to show the fallen, drawing figures running away and a flight of arrows as thick as the quills on a spine-back.

'Is this what I will do now?' Maia tossed aside the stick. 'Is this why Xania took me from the Cliff Village? To make war?'

'No. Xania was looking for a lost Sun Catcher.'

'The shaman called me a fire-bringer. And I have killed Wulf Kin. Taken my friends into battle.'

Her voice cracked. She turned away from the images. Watched the warriors and hunters tending their hurts, checking their horses and birds for wounds. Her own pony, its neck smeared with green heal-leaf, was cropping the grass nearby. Her fingers were still numb from where she had scooped up the mix to slather it over the scratches. Var had escaped with a few bruises and cuts. She was unhurt. Others had not been so lucky.

'I have caused this.'

'You did not send the Wulf Kin to attack Altara,' said Tareth. 'Elin and Urteth did.'

'Because of me,' said Maia.

'You didn't start this,' protested Tareth.

'But it started because of what I am.'

Tareth shook his head. 'It began when Elin killed your sisters and took the throne.'

Maia pointed at the sun figure image in the ashes. 'This isn't Elin. She's not the Sun Catcher.'

Tareth frowned at the drawing. 'Surely this tells an old story?' He examined the small figures beyond the flaming disc. 'Those are children. A family? And who's to say that the fire-bringer isn't bringing peace to the warriors? That this shows a far-has-been when tribes fought each other and this Sun Catcher, if that is what she is, ending the battle.'

Maia realised that he was trying to comfort her. She

wished she could believe his reasoning. But the shaman had been so sure about the story in the rock painting.

'There was more,' she said. 'Lost creatures. A rich land where there is now sand. The Kuma believe that the Sun Catcher burned the land. The shaman believes that I will bring war again.'

Tareth shook his head. 'I've never heard of these Kuma,' said Tareth. 'If their stories are true, then Xania would have heard them. The story-coat would have sung them. How can a land become sand?'

'Sun-fire destroys.'

'It brings light. An end to wolf-walk. New life. Not destruction.'

'I think it brings both,' said Maia. 'A Sun Catcher is a light-bringer. And a life-taker. Isn't that why you hid me away, kept silent? Never wanted me to discover what I was. Because I'm dangerous. Because I bring death.'

'No. I believed . . . Xania believed . . . that you were in danger, that Elin would kill you as she had killed her sisters so that she could be Queen. Elin thought that she would become the Sun Catcher.'

Maia sighed. 'But I became the Catcher and caught the sun.' She smoothed the ashes until there was no trace of the images. She wished it was as easy to rub out her knowledge. 'I thought that all would be well if I returned with silk and found a Story Singer. But I've failed. And there will be more fighting. And more death.'

Maia sat and brooded. War was not an answer. There had to be another way. Elin wanted power for herself, and she wanted Caspia to be queen after her. If Maia agreed to stand aside, to make Caspia the Story Singer, perhaps that would be enough to satisfy Elin and stop the fighting.

She could leave the Sun Palace to explore the mountains with the Eagle Hunters. Even brave the sun-deeps with Kodo and Trader Bron. Learn to live like the Kuma in the harsh beauty of their land. Watch the moths in the tree. Learn their secrets. They too could make silk for Tareth. She glanced at Var, who was cleaning his knives, murmuring to them. She could go with him to Azbarak's village of children. Everywhere she went she could still search for the new Story Singer – if Caspia wasn't the one to master the story-coat.

Kodo would reach the safety of the Sun City. Tareth would be able to make a moth-garden. She would help. He would weave new silk. And since Khandar needed a Sun Catcher, she would promise to return each solstice to catch the sun so that the land didn't fail.

The stick she had been stabbing into the ground broke. Tareth would never weave silk for Elin. He would never agree that Caspia was to become the Story Singer and wear Xania's coat.

Maia tossed the broken ends of stick away, narrowly missing Tiki who was nibbling the leather ties of Var's abandoned running blades. He squeaked, alerting Var, who started berating him.

Maia left them to squabble and went to find Egon. He was waiting at the edge of the encampment where he had been helping the archers make the travois on which to drag the injured who could not walk or ride to the Sun City. He was staring into the distance. As Maia approached he cast Garha into the sky.

'A rider. With an eagle,' he explained, watching Garha fly low and fast and then gain height so that she would soar above the incoming horseman and his bird.

Maia waited with him. 'More trouble?'

'He rides fast. See how his eagle stays close. Flies low above him.'

As he spoke the eagle abandoned the rider, climbed swiftly and powered towards Gahra. The two eagles met, spiralled together and, wingtips almost touching, flew towards Egon.

'It's Huan,' said Egon. 'I left him watching the Tower of Eagles.' He vaulted onto his pony and rode to meet his son.

Var joined Maia as she stood in a fret of impatience waiting for the pair to return. He had strapped on his running blades, ready to bound after Egon.

Maia placed her hand on his arm. 'Egon's son. Bringing messages.'

Var nodded, his eyes narrowed, scanning the grasslands. 'He's alone.' He removed his blades.

Yet Huan was riding as if pursued, thought Maia. His message must be bad.

It was worse than Maia feared.

'Kodo? You must be mistaken!' she insisted. 'He's with the Kuma, on the way to the city.'

Huan shook his head. The wide smile with which he had greeted her was gone.

'I saw him with my own eyes. He rode with the red witch's daughter and a Wulf Kin. They joined Urteth. Rode together to the tower.'

'Caspia?' gasped Maia. 'He was with Caspia?'

Huan nodded. He glanced at his father. 'There were eagles.'

'With the Wulf Kin?'

'Two. They attacked.' He glanced at his bird, which sat on the ground glaring yellow-eyed at the bustle around her.

Yanna handed Huan a beaker of steaming chay. 'They attacked your eagle?'

'She was too strong. Too swift even though there were two of them.' He spat the dust of his ride from his mouth and gulped down the chay. 'The Wulf Kin are trying to fly eagles with their wulfen.'

'How can this be true?' demanded Yanna.

'My son has seen it,' bristled Egon. 'So have I. They think they will defeat the Eagle People, tear our eagles from the sky. They train them only to fight, not to hunt.'

'But Kodo?' asked Maia. 'You're sure you saw Kodo?'

'How could I not know him? Have I not ridden with him? Did we not go together to hunt for your eagle and find KiKya?' said Huan. 'He was with them.'

'They must have captured him. Caught him crossing the plains to the city. He's their prisoner.'

'I thought so too. I didn't want to see what I saw. But he

rode freely, and was greeted by Urteth.'

'What did you see?' asked Var.

Huan looked at his feet, then in the air. He tried to be fair to his friend, tried to recall exactly what he had seen.

'He rode behind the flame-haired girl. Held her. Her arm was bound. Her tunic torn. The Wulf Kin was beside him. Silver bands gleamed on the Wulf Kin's arm. Kodo led another pony. Black. Beautiful. It favoured one foot. There was a bag on his shoulders. No eagles. They came later with Wulf Kin and a man in a wolfskin, their leader, Urteth. They rode together into the Tower of Eagles.' He opened his eyes and looked at Maia, his gaze dark with regret. 'I don't think he was a captive,' he said.

'He must be,' said Maia. 'He would never have gone to Caspia. He would never have given her the cocoons, and the last of the silk.'

CHAPTER TWENTY-THREE

If he stood on tiptoe, Kodo could hook his fingertips over the edge of the arrow slit and pull himself up. Wind whistled through the opening, making his eyes water as he pressed his face against the narrow gap. He could see sky. Distant mountains. Huge wings swept past. The shock made him lose his hold and he scraped his hands as he slid down the wall. He spat on his stinging skin. At least the opening let in a little light. He could explore his prison.

Sleeping furs lay jumbled in a corner. There was a pitcher of water. A bowl with the remains of a dried-up stew. A half-eaten flatbread. He wolfed the food down and quenched his thirst. The grumbling in his belly was no longer hunger. Now it was just anxiety. It wasn't much of an improvement. But he was no longer mind-mazed or frozen with fear.

The door was easy to open. A Wulf Kin lounged against

the doorframe, picking his pointed teeth with the tip of a knife. He snarled. Kodo shut the door. So not all Wulf Kin blades were poisoned as Maia had claimed. It made the beasts a little less fearsome. A little less lethal.

He should be grateful he was alive. Caspia must have told her parents that he had helped her. But he couldn't rid himself of the thought that he'd been foolish not to have tried to overwhelm the single Wulf Kin who rode with Caspia and to have escaped then. Caspia had stopped him. And she had taken his knife. Led him to her father and Elin, who was sure to remember that he'd stormed the Sun Palace with Tareth to find Maia. Then she would kill him.

In his mind, he could hear Caspia, talking about lizards and see her playing with a tiny blue one. He watched it change colour. Saw her smile at him and hold up the lizard. His silk dangled from its jaws. He reached out. And slapped his forehead. Hard. The jolt brought tears but broke the dream. She wasn't here in this room. Somehow Caspia was in his head.

He knew that Caspia would come to find him. The healer would set her bone, give her a potion to take away the pain, to make her sleep. But when she woke she would come. And she would ask him about the silk. Ask him where he had found it. But Maia had destroyed the moth-garden. There was no more silk. Only the scraps he carried in the back-sack and the silk she wore.

Maia had said she was taking the silk to Tareth with the moth eggs and cocoons so that he could make a new garden and breed moon-moths. Then he would weave silk. Kodo knew that was what the silk wanted. Tareth must weave silk.

The silk took away choice. As it had done when he had stolen it.

Kodo spread out a sleeping fur and emptied the small bundles from the back sack on to it. Carefully he unwrapped the packets and freed the old silk.

Maia was fighting a losing battle.

'I sent Kodo into danger. I will free him.'

'No,' said Tareth again.

Egon fed a tidbit to Garha. 'Urteth has broken our bond with the eagles. I will go with you.'

'The archers will ride with you,' added Yanna.

'It's a trap,' protested Tareth. 'Elin and Urteth are using the boy as bait to lure Maia to the Tower.'

'Var and I will go alone,' said Maia. 'We can find Kodo.'

'No.'

'If Kodo is a captive, then I'll come with you to rescue him,' announced Huan. 'I should have tried to warn him of danger when he rode into the Tower of Eagles.'

'You saw what you saw,' said Tareth. 'We don't know how Kodo met with Urteth. Or what will happen to him in the Tower. Kodo has the silk. We don't know what he will do with it.'

'Nothing,' said Maia. 'I shouldn't have sent him on alone.'

'The Wulf Kin attacked Altara,' Yanna clenched her fists. 'Elin sent them. They cower together like nesting rats thinking they are safe in the tower. We will flush them out.'

Egon grunted in agreement. 'I will summon the Eagle Hunters.'

'I know my brother,' continued Tareth. 'Urteth has been planning his return to the Sun City. Now Elin has joined him, he'll attempt to overthrow Maia so that Elin can again be Queen. He'll fight to destroy Maia here from his stronghold in the mountains. He has been waiting, gathering Wulf Kin, eagles, wulfen. We cannot attack the Tower. We are too few.'

'We have the Catcher.'

'No.' Tareth thumped his fist against his thigh. 'It is too dangerous.'

'And the Catcher has sun-fire,' continued Yanna. 'They cannot stand against her fire. Urteth has already felt its anger.'

The words were a child's chant, like the ones the weed children had sung in the weed beds, thought Maia. Those had been about the sun-deeps and harvesting the weed. Her lips framed the words as she remembered and imagined herself in the caves, swaying to the rhythm of the voices learning the way of the weed lore.

'Green, red, brown. Brown in the dark-deeps;
red in the sun-deeps; and always green near the shore.'

Did the children in Khandar sing about sun-fire and Sun Catchers?

Looking round the faces of her friends, their eyes bright with a mix of strong emotions, she realised that her homeland bred a fierce people. The weed people were hardy but they weren't ferocious. She couldn't imagine Laya relishing battle as Yanna did, nor Razek the Weed Master longing to launch the weed boys into an attack on the Marsh Lord's stronghold as Egon clearly wanted his tribe to do at the Tower.

'No,' said Tareth again. 'You don't know what you're asking.'

Maia remembered the fire roaring through her as she lost control and was consumed, blinded by light and flames. It still terrified her. She would never forget slaying the wulfen to save Kodo. It was fire made from rage and fear. Sun-fire caught in the sun-stone was easier to bear.

'I'll go with Var,' she told them. 'Speak with Urteth. And while I do, Var will find Kodo, smuggle him from the tower.'

'Tiki will find him. But what if the lizard boy doesn't wish to come?' Var asked.

'End his worthless life,' snapped Yanna.

'He'll come,' said Maia firmly. 'I know he will.'

'This is madness,' said Tareth. 'Do you think they will listen? Elin wants to be rid of you. Do you think she and Urteth will let you walk away? They'll kill you.'

'I will help her,' said Var.

'Guard her with one hand, while rescuing Kodo with the other? From the Wulf Kin and their beasts?' snapped Tareth. 'From my warrior brother and her witch sister? If anyone goes alone to the Tower of Eagles it will be me. Urteth is my brother. This is between us.'

'You can't–' Maia started to protest.

Tareth silenced her with a look. 'What can't I do? Rescue a boy who saved me from the sun-deeps? Outwit my twin? Protect you as I promised Xania I would when I snatched you from your cradle in the burning palace?'

His eyes were as sharp as an eagle's, his voice as unyielding as stone.

'I was a Warrior Weaver before I fell from the cliffs and needed sticks to walk. I hunted with eagles. Fought when the Wulf Kin attacked our village. Urteth and I did battle together. Entered the service of the Queen, your mother, together. But I was her Warrior Weaver. As I am yours, Sun Catcher. It is my place, my right, to ride to the Tower of Eagles and challenge my brother. I claim that right,' he finished fiercely. 'You will not deny me this.'

Maia felt as if the world had stilled. As if the ground had vanished from beneath her feet. As if the sun was falling from the sky.

She took a deep breath and knew she was going to deny him his demand. She must. He would die.

Tareth smiled at her. 'I owe Kodo my life, Maia. I will barter for his with my brother, Urteth.'

She heard a voice and realised that it was her own. 'Then we must make a plan to save Kodo and the silk.'

Kodo held the torn strip. The silk was old. The voices faint. The pictures tattered and frayed. But the story was still strong.

He saw a boy with an eagle. A girl riding towards a mountain village. She shone in the sunlight as if she was made of bronze yet, like her companions, she wore furs, a woven tunic, high boots. Her hair was the

colour of beech trees at leaf-fall. Her horse gleamed like copper tokens.
The silk loved her. She was laughing as she watched the boy showing off
his eagle's skill. She looked out of the dream at him.

In his eagerness to see more, Kodo touched the silk. It murmured and
the mind picture vanished. Another appeared. The same children, taller,
older, alone in a room. Kodo recognised it. They were in the Sun Palace.
The boy was arguing. He wore an eagle feather in his hair. Held a stick
bound with coloured thread in his hand. The girl shimmered.

Kodo sat back on his heels as he realised whose story the
silk was telling. The boy was Tareth. The silk whispered and
he saw the girl again, a billowing, cloud swirling about her
as she rode. She was singing. The silk coat she wore was
singing.

Kodo dreamed. Woke with his hands crushing the fragile
silk, his face wet. He groaned with a sense of terrible loss.
He knew that the loss was not his, but something felt by the
tattered pieces of silk worn so thin by the winds that swept
across the sun-deeps and battered the moth-garden that it
was almost transparent.

The old silk from the moth-garden told the tale of
Xania, the Story Singer, and Tareth. A story that was torn,
unfinished. A story in the silk that someone had ripped into
strips to hang on the thorn bushes in the garden where the
moon-moths flew. A story that kept the moths captive in
the secret garden. It had shown him a has-been that he must
keep safe.

He had to protect this silk. Caspia would tell them he
had it. He would be searched. Panic robbed him of breath.
The room seemed darker. The arrow slit was black like the
centre of a lizard's eye. How long had he been dreaming?

He listened but could hear nothing. He must hide the silk and conceal his pack before they came for him. No. They would know that he had hidden it. He must let them find something.

His stomach twisted at the thought of sacrificing some of the precious silk to keep the rest safe. Fingers trembling he opened the bundles. His thoughts darted like minnows in the shallows. He muttered the chant he used when he stole wild lizard eggs, hoping that, like the lizards, the ancient silk would forgive his betrayal.

Kodo chose a piece of silk that felt thicker than the rest and hid it in his boot with the torn strip. He must not surrender Xania and Tareth's song. He gathered the tumbled cocoons and wrapped some, trying to use the thinnest silk and tucked them in his tunic for Caspia to find. She would expect him to have some. But, he had to try to save most of the cocoons and eggs as well. He knotted a few in a fragile strip and slipped it into his back-sack. Fumbling in haste, he retied the last of the silk, tiny eggs and cocoons, making small bundles. He scrabbled across the room, seeking crevices and hollows in walls and floor. He heard voices. Desperately he shoved the silk out of sight.

The door opened.

CHAPTER TWENTY-FOUR

Urteth drained his beaker. The drink was dark and bitter, filling his mouth with the taste of leaf-fall wood fires and sour fruits. 'The boy is a liar.'

He watched the Wulf Kin drinking and eating close to the fire in the centre of the cold stone hall. The tusked pigs in the forests would make less noise as they grunted and rooted up the brown root fungus they loved. He felt his half-hand twitch as if he held his boar spear. He wanted to hunt. He would ride out at sun-wake. Take Zartev. Chase pigs.

He roared at the Wulf Kin lounging closest to the fire as they gorged on the snow cat whose long-tailed pelt now hung in the tower's cellars. It would make a fine saddlecloth. He shouted at them to throw more wood on the blaze. He was cold. Not even the wolfskin he had slung across his shoulders kept out the chill that lodged in his bones since he had been burnt by the sun-stone.

'The boy's story is a tangle of lies. You will have to unpick it, daughter. He wriggles like a fish on a line, and tells me what I know must be true, and yet beneath the water he hides something. He is a trader – yet more. He is on land – yet sails on the far-deeps. He trembles with fear – yet answers boldly. He is not what he seems. '

He refilled his beaker from a brimming pottery jug and drank deeply.

Elin glanced at him, her face pinched, her eyes sharp. 'He will not lie to me.'

'Nor me,' said Caspia. She smiled as she thought about her easy conquest of the boy who loved lizards and gold and silk.

She pulled a wing from the baked goose lying in a puddle of fat on the platter Zartev had placed on the huge table. Its skin gleamed like bronze with grease. Her mouth watered. She was starving. Her stomach growled. She tore the flesh from the bone and realised as she forced herself to swallow the baked meat that the hunger wasn't hers. She was catching the boy's thoughts.

She threw the goose leg aside and tugged back her thought-stealing tentacles. They resisted. They had a mind of their own, refusing to obey, seeking thoughts she hadn't asked them to find. His thoughts, his hunger. It overwhelmed her.

'He's hungry. We must feed him,' she said impulsively. She lifted her hand to summon Vultek. The Wulf Kin ignored her.

Caspia felt a flash of anger and lost contact with the boy's hunger pangs.

'Feed him maggots,' said Urteth. 'He has a taste for those.'

'Maggots!' The goose grease in her mouth made her feel sick. Caspia reached for a handful of berries. Their sharp sweetness took away the taste of roasted flesh.

'Cocoons,' Urteth corrected himself. 'He collects them for his master.' He pulled his wolf-pelt closer round his shoulders. 'He claims they are good for sun-deep chills.'

'He has cocoons?' asked Elin.

'To bake and pound into a powder, if he's to be believed,' said Urteth.

Caspia cast her thought-stealing net again. 'He growls with hunger. He's always hungry. His thoughts are so strong it makes me want to eat. I'll hear nothing until he stops groaning.'

Elin twisted the ring on her thumb. 'Your brother was the Queen's Weaver. He needs silk. The palace garden is dead, burned by your Wulf Kin when Tareth stole the sun-stone. Now he's returned to the palace he'll need moths.' She glared at Urteth. 'The boy has fooled you. The maggots are not food for his master.

'If he thinks only of his belly, take him food. Let him feast until he's overcome by the taste and smell of baked meats, dazed by warm honeyed vine juices, and thinks only of the sweet, sticky flatbreads still to eat. Then enter his mind and find the truth,' she told Caspia.

She beckoned to Zartev. 'Fetch food for the boy. Let him eat and drink. Then take Caspia to him.'

She turned to Urteth.

'The Weaver is nothing without silk. We have the story-coat. Now we have the boy. He'll take us to the moth-garden and we will have the makings of new silk.' Her hands stroked the band of silk on her gown. 'And we can drown Xania's coat and rid ourselves of its memories and lies.

'We have no need of its tales. Xania the Story Singer is dead. Her stories are dead. Tales of the has-been,' said Elin. 'We'll make new stories. Caspia will wear new silk.'

'And who will weave this new silk?' demanded Urteth.

Elin laughed. 'The Warrior Weaver. He will beg us to give him the cocoons. And if he cannot be persuaded to help us then we'll search and find a new weaver. Isn't that how my mother found her silk-maker when none of my sisters was able to work the whispering silk?'

Urteth nodded slowly. 'The search came to our village when we were young. Tareth was chosen to weave the silk for Xania the Story Singer. But I know my brother. He'll never weave for you.

Elin shrugged. 'Then he can die with the Sun Catcher.'

Caspia glowered at the back of the Wulf Kin as she followed him. If her mother was so keen on finding new silk she should speak to the lizard boy herself. There would be no need for thought-stealing then. There were other ways to make the boy speak. She yawned and wished she was snuggled deep in her sleeping furs. Sun-wake would have been soon enough to visit the boy.

But Elin hadn't listened to her protests. She was desperate

for any scrap of silk, which was strange since she seemed to fear it. She wouldn't hold the tattered piece the boy had given her. She rarely stroked the silk band woven into her gown as if she no longer found comfort in its whispers.

Zartev, her father's loyal companion, was waiting for her.

'The boy has eaten,' he said. 'And asked for more.'

'Then send for more,' said Caspia. 'He has a sweet tongue,' she said, frowning as she was bombarded by Kodo's thoughts. 'Blueberry flatbreads, warm from the bake stone, shared with friends.' The image was so bright she could almost feel the juice spill down her chin.

She opened the door, took the flaming brand from the Wulf Kin and placed it in the metal ring in the wall.

Kodo blinked in the sudden dazzle of light. He watched as Caspia, in her blue gown, a jewel gleaming on her hand, crossed the room. She smiled.

CHAPTER TWENTY-FIVE

Caspia dropped the bag the lizard boy had given her on her mother's sleeping furs.

'He was hiding this.'

The haul was disappointing. A few bundles of dried leaves and cocoons. A drift of eggs tied in a strip of torn cloth. Two small pieces of tattered silk tucked in the bottom of the bag. A piece of bark, an empty water pouch and one shiny brown bead.

Elin tipped out the contents of the bag. 'Only this?'

Caspia shrugged. 'It's all he had.'

'Where did he find the silk?'

'Far from here. I saw sun-deeps. A cliff.' She pointed to the brown bead. 'Is that the baked cocoon he told you about?'

Urteth crossed to the sleeping platform. He rolled the bead across his palm, broke it open with his fingernail. 'A maggot.' Ignoring Elin's warning hiss, he tasted it with the tip of his tongue. 'Perhaps it was not all lies.'

Elin avoided touching the silk as she examined a leaf wrapping. 'What else did you see, daughter?'

Caspia grimaced. 'Lizards. Fish. Food on a bakestone. A woman. A storm. Stars. Sun-deeps. And flatbread. Lots and lots of baked flatbread.'

Urteth returned to the arrow slit. 'Stars.'

'To find his way.'

'A woman?' asked Elin.

'His mother, cooking.' Caspia toyed with her thumb ring. 'And another. As old as the mountains. She looked like a crow. She scares him. His thoughts are as tangled as wulfen fur.'

Urteth laughed. 'Did his thoughts bore you, daughter?'

Caspia shrugged and yawned. 'He thinks like a child telling stories to keep away the dark.'

Elin stared at Kodo's few possessions scattered on the sleeping furs. 'And yet he carries silk.'

She rose from the sleeping platform, wrapping a thick fur-lined cloak around her shoulders. 'I will see him.'

Kodo curled into a ball and buried his head in his arm. He had never felt so alone.

Caspia had gone, taking the back-sack with her. Kodo stifled a groan. What else had she stolen while he was mind-mazed?

He fumbled inside his tunic. The packet he'd hidden there was gone. How had she found that? He'd been so sure that he had blocked his thoughts, thinking of the feast he had just eaten. It had been easy to do that. To share the sticky flatbreads the Wulf Kin had brought. She had laughed when the fruit juice spurted down his chin, just as Maia always did.

Kodo bit his fist. He'd betrayed Maia who had trusted him to take the cocoons to the Sun City. Betrayed the silk. Betrayed them with his greed as he gobbled blueberry flatbreads. He must have grown careless and let down his guard. He would never eat blueberry flatbread again.

He heard footsteps. Caspia's Wulf Kin companion loomed in the doorway.

'Come,' growled Vultek.

Kodo tried not to breathe in the overpowering stench of fur and oiled leather, sweat and grease as the Wulf Kin pushed him up the stone stairs spiralling through the narrow tower.

He hit his knee on the stone step and bit back a cry. He tasted salt and blood. He could hear voices above.

A woman, her words sharp and clear with excitement. Elin. He shivered.

'Altara defeated!'

'Burned to the ground. The last of the Warrior Women are besieged, surrounded by Wulf Kin,' rumbled a deeper voice. 'They cannot escape. All will die as you commanded, my Queen.'

Kodo froze. His thoughts scurried like a lapran seeking its burrow as a hawk swooped. Had Maia reached Altara before it burned? Had she been trapped there? Was she hurt?

He didn't feel the Wulf Kin's shove.

'Yanna and her archers betrayed us,' said Elin. 'Altara will be a warning to any who stand against me.'

'The Sun City will not stand against you.'

Kodo recognised Urteth's voice.

'It will not dare,' agreed Elin. 'Azbarak is too fond of his skin to stand against me. The Keeper will open the gates and welcome me when he learns of Altara's fate.'

'You think Azbarak will betray the Sun Catcher?'

'He knows where his loyalty lies. The city is as good as ours once Azbarak sees the Wulf Kin riding with me. Azbarak does what is best for Azbarak.'

'The Catcher's supporters won't surrender the city and the stone without a fight.'

Kodo stumbled into the room. He was aware of four pairs of eyes watching him. Caspia smiled and he felt her deftly harvesting his thoughts.

'The Sun Catcher can't defend the city,' said Caspia. 'She isn't there.'

'Then where is she?' demanded Elin.

'Will you tell them? Or shall I?' Caspia's voice caressed him.

Kodo trembled with the effort to keeps his lips shut tight and to think of nothing. He tried to break the contact with Caspia's bright blue eyes. Eyes like the sky. Like the sun-deeps where the lizards were swimming, plunging into the breaking tops of the waves, playing in the flying spray, tumbling him over and over in the cool water.

'You are the boy with silk?' In a swirl of fur, Elin strode towards him.

Her eyes were like fire. He would be skewered and roasted. Kodo knew he'd tell her anything she asked just to escape her fury. He glanced at Caspia, begging her silently to save him.

'He is the boy who gave me the old silk. Who pulled me from the pit.'

'He came to the Sun Palace,' remembered Elin. 'He came armed to attack me. He came to find the Sun Catcher. To protect her.'

'I saw him at Haddra,' Urteth frowned at Kodo, 'when I searched the harbour for the Story Singer and the girl. He was aboard the last boat to reach Haddra before the rivers froze.'

'He was there,' confirmed the old Wulf Kin.

'And my brother Tareth was with you,' guessed Urteth. 'I felt him near. He was on the boat. You went with him to the Sun Palace, now you carry the silk he needs to make another moth-garden. You're no trader.'

'I am a trader,' stuttered Kodo. 'My master is Bron.'

'The Catcher is his friend,' said Caspia. 'He was journeying with her.'

Elin's nails raked the silk on her gown. 'Maia has left the city.'

Caspia nodded. She looked at Kodo. 'She left you alone and abandoned the city. You watched her leave. She went to Altara.'

Elin laughed. The sound sent a chill along Kodo's spine.

'Then she is dead and the city and the sun-stone are mine. I will ride at sun-wake. Enter the city. Claim the sun-stone.'

Urteth caressed the bronze wrist sleeve covering his damaged hand.

He nodded. 'Go to the city. Claim the sun-stone for Caspia. Once the Wulf Kin return from Altara we'll ride to join you.

'Before wolf-walk our daughter will be the new Sun Catcher and you will rule again as Queen.'

CHAPTER TWENTY-SIX

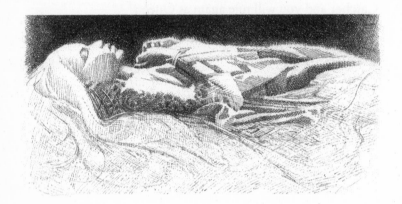

Caspia ordered the Wulf Kin to walk several paces behind them. Kodo caught the scent of Caspia's hair and gown. Summer grass, flowers, a hint of the water-leaf that his mother picked to place in the baby's cradle to help her sleep.

He felt the soft, stealthy probe as Caspia netted his thoughts. He decided he didn't care if she stole his memories again. Thoughts of the Stilt Village, his home, his family were safe. Caspia couldn't do any harm if she twisted those things from him.

He wiped his nose on the back of his hand. He wouldn't believe that Maia was gone. He'd think about her and her story-telling as she stood in a puddle of blue and gold cloth and wove half-truths about her encounter with lizards. Remember how she'd defended the eagle who had killed a hatchling and made him a hero for battling with the fierce bird. He would tell her tale, sing it to whoever would listen.

'She was there? The Sun Catcher? She grew up with lizards? With you?' Caspia laughed. 'I didn't know that my mother fears a lizard girl.'

Kodo stopped abruptly, fists clenched. 'You know nothing!'

Caspia smiled. 'I know what I hear. I know about your lizards. About the Catcher who loves silk more than her friends. I know what you've told me.'

'I didn't tell you! You stole my thoughts. I thought you were my friend, but what friend does that?'

Caspia watched him warily. 'I am your friend. Vultek, the Wulf Kin, would have killed you. I stopped him.'

'You took my knife. I would have stabbed him and his wulfen.'

'And ridden into the arms of Urteth and the Wulf Kin with Vultek's blood on your blade. Not even my father would have listened to me then. I couldn't have saved you.'

'You lied to me. Tricked me into trusting you. I gave you my silk.'

'To show my mother. To let her see how you helped me.'

Kodo shook his head to clear his thoughts. Her voice was like honey. Her face sweet, her words reasoned.

He clung to his grievance like a drowning man grasping a floating oar.

'You are a thief. A thought-thief. A silk-thief.'

Her eyes were like the blue ice deep in the frozen rivers of wolf-walk.

'I kept you safe,' said Caspia 'I'm tired of the Wulf Kin. They don't understand me. I thought you did. I wanted a friend. The silk likes you.'

Kodo almost believed her. No one would want a Wulf Kin as a companion.

'The silk likes me?' The thought filled him with wonder.

'Don't you hear it whisper?'

Kodo hesitated. 'Sometimes.'

'I wanted to listen to the memories the old silk told you.' She dropped her eyes. 'I wanted you to share the songs in the story-coat my mother has given me.'

'You have the story-coat?'

Caspia nodded. 'My mother brought it from the Sun Palace.'

Kodo felt the fog in his head roll away as if the wind blowing ashore with sea-rise had dispersed the ragged, curling drifts of mist.

He had seen the silk coat gleaming around Maia as she had stood in the Stone Square before she lifted the sun-stone and caught the sun. The coat was beautiful. It had belonged to her sister Xania. It was worn by the Sun Catcher when she caught the sun, but it belonged to the Story Singer. Elin had no right to take it. No right to give it to Caspia. She wasn't a Story Singer. He hadn't heard Caspia's voice in the silk.

He hoped Maia would approve of what he was going to do.

'I'd like to share the stories with you,' he said.

Caspia slipped into her mother's chamber. The room was empty. A felt saddlebag lay on the platform. A coat trimmed with fur, and purple woollen trousers had been tossed onto her sleeping furs, together with thigh-high boots. Clothes for a journey.

Caspia examined the saddlebag and discovered a small leather pouch holding her mother's amber beads, her hair comb with its enamelled leaping cat twined in a tangle of leaves, and a small pot with a lid which held the sweet-smelling paste of pounded cypress, cedar and frankincense wood Elin used to cleanse her skin. It was a large bag for such small things. Her mother was going to take the sun-helmet and the story-coat with her.

She glanced round the room and saw that the soft leather back-sack holding the coat lay half hidden beneath the sleeping platform. She pulled out the bag and sat with it on her knee. If her mother took the coat she would not be able to try out her plan. She slipped her hand inside the bag. The silk was cool. She rubbed it between her fingers. It didn't whisper.

She tugged the coat from the bag and flung it about her shoulders. The silk sighed as it tumbled in soft folds about her and then fell silent. She could sense it listening.

'I am Caspia,' she said. 'Daughter of Elin. I am to be Queen. Show me your stories. Sing to me.'

Nothing. Only a creeping chill in her fingers which held the coat. She opened her hands and the silk slipped from her shoulders.

'You cannot keep your secrets from me,' she hissed. 'They are mine by birthright. My mother's kin made you. The

183

stories are theirs and mine.' She bundled the coat back into the bag. 'I will find a Story Singer and I will hear your stories.'

She wanted to know what her mother had never told her. The tales of the has-been. She was a thought-stealer. If the silk wouldn't tell her she would capture the thoughts of another. She already had.

It was cold. Kodo shivered. The pungent smell of burning oil caught in the back of his throat. A woman with a face as white as sea foam was lying on a cloth of gold. She was wearing an embroidered coat, long deerskin boots. The silk was sad, weeping. He could hear the crack of cloth flapping in the wind, the rise and fall of a song so like the eerie death warble of his grandfather's lizards that it broke his heart. He felt flakes of snow land and melt on his lips. He thought he saw Maia, her head bowed. She didn't see him. Kodo tried to speak to her, but she just tugged an eagle feather from her hair and gave it to the woman, tucking it into the frayed silk band on her wrist.

He watched as Maia struggled to control the silk. It rippled under her hands. She bundled it under her arm as she turned away from the woman.

Kodo moved closer. It was Xania. The Story Singer.

The woman's dark eyes opened.

'Am I dreaming you, silk thief?' Her voice was soft, like moth wings brushing against him.

She seemed to look through and beyond him to be listening to something far away. She smiled. 'Silk thief,' she whispered. 'Story Singer. Listen to my story.'

'What do you see?' demanded Caspia. 'Did it sing to you?'

The silk slipped from Kodo's hands.

'Death,' he muttered.

He tried to banish the images, to focus on the plunge into the dark, the cold, the loss.

'Whose? My father's? Mine? My mother's?' asked Caspia fiercely.

'Sadness. The silk wept,' muttered Kodo.

'So you did hear it sing?'

Kodo nodded. 'It sang a death song.'

He looked directly at her and thought of the song he had heard. He knew he mustn't think of anything else until he was alone.

'It was an old song, faint, almost forgotten. Like a night-wake. It was the death song for a Story Singer.'

'Good,' said Caspia. 'The silk sings for you.'

She took the coat from him and bundled it into the bag to return it to Elin's chamber.

Kodo felt as if part of him had been torn away. It was all he could do not to snatch the bag from Caspia, to pull the silk from the stifling darkness, to slip his arms into the sleeves so that it fell like a waterfall and the tumbling cascade drowned him in its song. The silk knew him. It wanted him to sing. The coat was his. He choked back a sound that bubbled in his throat.

'You will tell me the stories in the coat.' Caspia's eyes blazed. 'The silk will give up its secrets.'

'Story Singer.' The whisper came from somewhere deep inside him, like a distant memory. Kodo's heart leapt. Then he felt it plummet like a gull brought down by a slingshot. The whisper must have been Caspia's. She was a dream-stealer, a thought-thief. She wanted the silk. She'd say anything to trick him into doing as she wished. He knew he couldn't be like Xania, Maia's sister. He was a silk-thief. He was a trader. He was the grandson of Ootey the Lizard Keeper.

'I'm only a lizard boy,' he said. And Maia's friend, he thought as he tried to block Caspia. He mustn't give her the silk's secrets.

She grinned at him. 'You're a liar, just as my father said. But the silk will make you sing the truth for me!'

CHAPTER TWENTY-SEVEN

Maia spread out her weapons. She tested the edge of the blade of her knife, carelessly slitting the skin on her thumb.

'Shells!' she muttered and sucked the split skin. She ignored the look Var sent her. He was never clumsy. She felt for the shoulder knife Tareth had given her when she had left the weed beds. It no longer nestled snugly beneath her tunic. For a moment she thought she had lost it. Then she remembered that she'd given it to Kodo.

'D'you think he's all right?' she asked Var.

Var didn't have to ask who she was thinking about.

'He's strong,' he answered as he had when she had asked before.

'He'll be so alone. Afraid.'

Var didn't reply. He wondered if the lizard boy still lived.

'He isn't like you. You choose to be alone.'

Var touched the two stones hidden in his tunic. The Watcher had told him he would have to choose many things.

'He'll think we have forgotten him,' said Maia.

'He decided not to fight with you.' Var slipped one of his knives into his boot. 'He was eager to leave with the Kuma.'

Maia thought she heard criticism in his voice. 'Kodo isn't afraid to fight . . . even if he isn't a trained . . .'

'Killer.' A tide of colour washed across Var's skin.

'Warrior,' said Maia. 'As we all are now. It's just . . . I'm afraid for him. He's Urteth's prisoner . . . If Elin is there and remembers him she'll punish him.'

Var adjusted the snug fit of the dagger sheath in his boot and waited. What she said was true. He knew that she would ask him to leave to find and rescue the boy.

She didn't.

'It's my fault. We should have stayed together. I shouldn't have let him take the silk and eggs,' said Maia. If she hadn't let him go on alone with the silk he wouldn't be in danger now. And Tareth and the archers and the Eagle Hunters wouldn't be preparing to ride to rescue him. They were risking their lives.

She nibbled her thumbnail. She wished she'd trusted Kodo and told him all that she knew about the silk. Then he would know what to do.

Kodo liked the silk. It didn't scare him as it sometimes frightened her with its stories. He'd been wrong to steal the silk, but it hadn't harmed him. Didn't torment him as it tormented Elin with her guilt. He'd gone unscathed into the moth-garden. Hadn't plugged his ears with beeswax as

Tareth had warned her she must. The silk must like Kodo.

The thought came suddenly, surprising her. She'd been so busy keeping the silk secret, being angry when Kodo had given in to temptation and stolen some from the moth-garden, worrying about protecting him because she knew the silk was dangerous, that she'd never thought about how the silk responded to him. He'd said that it made him dream, had shown him the to-come when he would sail with Trader.

Yells and a scuffle broke into her thoughts.

Huan, red-faced, breathless, lurched towards them with a struggling figure clamped under his arm. Yanna strode after him, followed by Egon.

'Keep still brat or I'll set my eagle on you,' gasped Huan.

The child wriggled harder. Slipped from Huan's grasp and landed on all fours close to Maia. Beneath shaggy hair bright eyes peered at her. Teeth bared in a fierce grimace, he tensed himself to run. Then he screeched, and sprang at Var.

Clinging to him like a monkey, the child pounded on his back, shrieking, 'Var! Var!'

Var staggered and set the boy on his feet.

He hopped in front of Var. 'Where's Tiki?'

Maia saw the rat's twitching nose and whiskers appear. The child crowed with delight, pulled something from his ragged tunic and tossed it the air. Before it tumbled to the ground Tiki slithered from Var's tunic to catch the prize.

Yanna hissed as the rat ran across her foot. Then she bent and picked up a small chunk of turquoise from the grass.

'My ear stud!'

She pointed at the boy. 'It fell from his belt pouch.' She made a grab for the boy and missed as he darted behind

Egon. The Eagle Hunter twisted to catch him and lost his balance. Huan threw himself forward to tackle the boy around the knees. The child evaded him, skipped past Maia and hid behind Var.

'The boy's a thief,' accused Yanna.

Var reached behind him and drew the boy forward.

'What are you doing here, Leeto?'

'Azbarak sent me.' The child pointed at Yanna. 'To find her and the man with the eagle.' He looked at Egon, then at Huan who was climbing to his feet. 'Not them. A man with sticks. Keeper wanted to know if they still lived.'

'We do, little thief, as you can see,' retorted Yanna. 'Did Azbarak also send you to rob us?'

'What have you stolen, Leeto?' asked Var.

The child nodded towards Yanna. 'Her blue stone. So that Azbarak would believe that I'd found her.'

Var waited. Leeto watched him with wide innocent eyes. Var held out his hand.

The boy's shoulders drooped. 'I wouldn't have taken them to the city.' He glanced at Yanna. 'Only hers. Azbarak likes blue stones.'

Leeto pulled a tiny horde of stolen objects from his clothes. Maia gasped as he spun them in the air, juggling them from hand to hand, tossing them over his head, catching them and spinning them high. Huan just managed to catch his bridle charm as the gleaming gold stag tumbled towards him. Egon's feathered eagle hood dropped into his lap. The healer's knife twisted towards Var. Leeto back-flipped across the firepit, took Maia's hand and laid three bone needles on her palm.

He was like Bojo, the long-tailed monkey who guarded Trader Bron's boat. Maia grinned.

'You're almost as good a juggler as my sister, Xania,' she said.

'Better,' insisted Leeto. 'I'm the best that the Keeper has ever found.'

'Jugglers as well as thieves and assassins,' said Yanna grimly. 'Who else has joined Azbarak in the city?'

Var ignored her. 'What did the Keeper tell you to do?' he asked.

'I'm to tell him what is happening at Altara,' said the boy.

'And what will you say?'

'That the Wulf Kin are gone. That Altara is no more. But that the archers will ride to the Tower of Eagles with the Eagle Hunters.'

'A small boy with big ears,' said Yanna. 'What else have you heard, thief?'

Leeto glanced at Var.

'She can know,' said Var. 'She's a friend.'

The boy looked doubtful. 'I'll tell him that the Sun Catcher is here. And that I have found Var.' He touched Var's hand. 'He's been searching for you.'

Var nodded.

'Does the Sun Catcher also go to the Tower of Eagles?' asked the boy. 'Do you go with her?'

Var hesitated. He'd promised Tareth that he would go to the Tower. Azbarak would expect him to return to the Sun City. He felt the tug of choices. He was no longer sure that his loyalty to the Keeper was strong.

'Var will return to the Sun Palace with me,' said Maia. 'Tell Azbarak that he must prepare the moth-garden. Say

191

that the Sun Catcher will reach the city soon.'

She thought of the task ahead. Thought of the decision she must make and wondered if she would ever return to the Sun City.

She watched Leeto depart. 'He's very young. Did he come alone?'

Var shrugged. 'Perhaps.'

But Leeto wasn't alone. As the boy ascended a slight rise she saw three short figures rise from the long grass to join him. They stood talking and then set off together across the grassland. Maia squinted at the sun and checked the direction of her shadow. The children were jogging towards the Sun City, taking news of Altara and her message to Azbarak. What else would they tell him?

Yanna had seen the group. 'I knew the boy had accomplices. The Keeper trains his little rats to hunt in packs.' She pushed her turquoise stud through the tiny hole in her earlobe. She glowered at Var. 'Why does Azbarak keep so many urchins? The Sun Palace is full of his children. What's he planning?'

'Azbarak's purposes are his own,' said Var. 'He tells us what to do, not why he wishes it.' He handed her the knife he held. 'Your healer will need this.'

'And her needles,' said Maia, setting off to find the grey-robed woman who was arranging to move the injured. She must speak to Tareth.

Yanna caught up with her. 'You've heard what the wounded are saying? That if they can walk or ride they are coming with us? Only the worst hurt have agreed to go to the Sun City.'

'You must persuade them to seek safety in the city,' Maia answered.

'They are warriors. Their cats will stay to fight with us. So will they.'

'We're going to find Kodo,' said Maia. 'Not to start a war. Tareth hopes Urteth will listen to him. And that he can persude him to release Kodo.'

'We're going to destroy rats in their nest so that they do not spread their evil throughout Khandar.' Yanna caught Maia's arm. 'Elin cannot be allowed to escape again. She's the sickness which infects us all. And the Wulf Kin support her. You know this. She must be stopped.'

Maia tugged her arm free. 'I tried. We fought. I couldn't kill her. She is my sister. I couldn't kill her.'

'Then send another to kill her,' said Yanna.

Maia shook her head. 'I can't ask someone else to do what I cannot.'

'You do not need to ask,' said Yanna. 'I will do it.'

'No.' Maia closed her fist around the bone needles she held.

She felt the points prick her palm like the almost-forgotten memory of the numbness in her hands when Elin's ring had flared blue and frozen her hand. She had dropped the knife, had watched it distort and melt. Her knives had been of no use against Elin until the sun-stone had drained her ring of light.

She couldn't call on the sun-stone here. It still gleamed high on the Catching stone, its power waning with the approach of wolf-walk. She knew that she was supposed to remove the stone and keep it safe until new-leaf.

She scuffed her foot against a tough tussock of grass, watching the tiny seed heads shake free from the yellowing stalks. She had to find a way to deal with Elin. A way which didn't send the Warriors and the Hunters into another battle while Elin waited like a spider in the centre of her web.

'She owes me many lives,' said Yanna. 'She sent the Wulf Kin to Altara. I do not fear her. I will send her into darkness.'

'I'm not afraid to fight Elin. I tried to use my fire against her. I couldn't.'

'You are the Sun Catcher. She cannot stand against you.'

'She did.'

'You caught the sun. She is no longer Queen.'

'Yet she still commands, still brings fear and pain. She and Urteth have summoned Wulf Kin. They attack those who stand against them.'

'You will be able to stop her.'

Maia wished she was as confident as Yanna. 'There will be a way,' she said slowly. There had to be.

And suddenly she knew what it was.

'You're mistaken. Kodo cannot be a Story Singer,' said Tareth.

'The silk calls to him.'

'He's a lizard boy. A trader.'

'That too,' agreed Maia. 'And Xania was a warrior and a juggler, as well as a Story Singer.'

'You told me you thought Caspia was the Story Singer. Now you say it's Kodo. Neither can take Xania's place.'

'You tasked me with finding a Story Singer. Caspia can

hear thoughts, catch dreams. She is like the silk . . . But it speaks to Kodo. He can hear his lizards sing . . . I think he can listen to the silk's stories. It's already whispered to him.'

'He's the Lizard Master's grandson,' protested Tareth. 'A good friend, but he knows nothing of Khandar or silk. He'd never seen any until he followed you to the moth-garden and stole it.'

'And I knew nothing of Khandar. I'd never seen the sunstone. Yet I am the Sun Catcher,' said Maia.

'Your mother was Queen and Sun Catcher. All of her daughters, your lost sisters, had power. Xania became the Story Singer. You are the Sun Catcher. Kodo is a fine boy. He dreams of becoming a trader. It's the Queen and her family who tend the moths, make the silk, sing its stories.'

'Yet none could weave the silk. Only you. The son of an Eagle Hunter.'

Tareth paused, his arguments dying on his lips. 'Xania found me on a search when she listened to the silk,' he said slowly.

'And Xania has no daughter to wear the coat,' Maia tried not to see how her words hurt him. 'The silk hasn't chosen me. We need a Story Singer.

'Kodo can hear the silk whisper. Just as you could, although you were the son of the mountains not the Sun City.'

Tareth shook his head. 'Surely the silk would have told me. Has your silk spoken to you about Kodo.'

'My silk has never sung,' Maia reminded him reluctantly. 'But I know Kodo listens to the silk. It sings for him. If he's not a Singer, then who is?'

'It's true that Kodo heard the silk in Haddra when he

climbed the white watchtower,' remembered Tareth. 'Perhaps you're right. The old silk he carries to Khandar will know. It will have listened to him and learned what he is. '

'I'm afraid for him,' said Maia. 'He is with Caspia. She is a thought-thief. She may discover the truth. And if she can't hear the silk stories she will make Kodo sing for her.'

CHAPTER TWENTY-EIGHT

Kodo hung from the edge of the arrow slit and hauled himself up until he was high enough to peer through it. His shoulders creaked with the effort as he clung to the granite like a sucker-toed gecko.

He could see tops of heads, red hair, matted Wulf Kin fur, a black wolfskin hat. Ponies milled in the enclosed yard, among long-legged hunting hounds and a pack of wulfen. He saw a flaming head above a blue tunic and boots toss a fur-trimmed coat across the saddle of a black pony.

Caspia. Leaving with her mother and a large escort. Now Altara had fallen, Elin must be riding to the Sun City. If only he could warn them.

He crossed to the door and tried the latch. It was fastened. He was a prisoner. Caspia had abandoned him to the horde of Wulf Kin still guarding the Tower. He wondered how long he would have before they remembered him.

No one came. Despite his determination to stay alert, Kodo dozed. A faint noise disturbed him. Something trailed across his face, ran down his chest and over his hand. Kodo jerked awake. A rat. He hated rats. He could hear scrabbling. He pulled off his boot, and threw it at the sound. He heard a squeak as the boot hit the wall. Then a flicker as a shadow scurried across the floor, ran up the wall and vanished through the arrow slit. As he picked up his boot he glanced. A black rat crouched above him. The tail was crooked. It was Tiki.

'Var?' he called softly. 'Var.'

The darkness was silent and still.

Then the latch lifted. The door opened. Kodo sprang forward as a figure lurched into the room and found himself struggling with a Wulf Kin who slid through his arms and collapsed at his feet.

Var slipped into the room.

'Come,' he whispered. 'Quietly.'

Kodo pulled on his boot. 'Is Maia all right? They said Altara burned.'

'She is safe. Come.'

'Wait,' Kodo dropped to his knees, running his hands across the bottom course of stones in the wall, found the loose one and worked it free. He pulled a bundle from the hiding place and tucked it inside his tunic. He crawled across the floor retrieving his tiny hoard.

Var was dragging the body from the room. Kodo helped him prop it against the wall. Var folded the Wulf Kin's arm, arranged his legs. Realising what he was doing, Kodo fetched his empty bowl and placed it beside the slumped figure.

'Looks like he's drunk or sleeping,' he hissed.

Var's fingers dug painfully into his arm. 'Stay in the shadows.'

They had nearly reached the steps when they heard footsteps and the chink of mail, and saw the leaping shadow cast by a flaming torch coming towards them. Kodo tugged Var into a doorway. The door gave way and they fell into the room behind it. Kodo lay still, scarcely daring to breathe. Var eased the door shut. They heard someone ascend the spiral stair. Light gleamed beneath the door.

Kodo held his breath. Var slipped his knife from its sheath.

'Urteth?' someone called

Kodo tugged at Var's tunic. 'Can we escape from the roof? Did you bring a rope?'

Var shook his head.

'Pity,' Kodo glanced round the room. 'Best to wait until they sleep.'

Var reached into his belt pouch and handed Kodo a shard of burned wood. 'We will be caught like birds in a throw-net if we stay here. Smear your face and hands, it will be better if we hide in the shadows below.'

Kodo did as he was told and almost cried out as his finger was bitten. In the dimness he saw Tiki sitting on Var's hand, gnawing the end of the stick. He quelled the urge to knock the rat across the room.

'Did he have to bite me?' he hissed. 'He's drawn blood.'

Var's teeth shone white. 'A small payment for finding you. He'll also lead us out of here.'

He set the rat on the floor. 'He'll show us if the way is clear.'

To Kodo's surprise Tiki scurried from the room and Var settled himself cross- legged on the floor and closed his eyes. Wondering how Var could seem so calm, Kodo tried to copy him. It was no use. He jangled with tension. He stood. Paced the room. Sat. Paced again. He heard Var sigh.

Kodo checked that the bundles were still safe in his tunic. He tightened his belt, tried to sit still. His thoughts spun in circles like fish in a keep-net.

Finally Var stirred. 'Come,' he said.

The fire was low, white ash dropping from spent logs. No one had replaced the torches in the hollowed stone brackets. A Wulf Kin snored close to the hearth. A wulfen stretched near the door which led to the outside. They would never get past the animal.

Kodo glanced at Var, willing him to kill the beast.

Var beckoned Kodo to follow and slipped into the shadows, moving soft-footed until they were close enough to the door to hear the beast grumbling in its sleep.

Kodo was unable to take his eyes from the wulfen. He saw Tiki leap onto its head, scamper along its nose and bite hard.

The wulfen woke, roared and shook his giant head to dislodge the rat clamped on his nose. Tiki flew through the air. The rat twisted and landed on all fours. The wulfen launched forward but Tiki raced towards the dais and leapt onto Elin's chair.

Var sprinted to the door and vanished into the dark. Kodo heard a thump. There was a yell as the Wulf Kin woke. He thought he heard Tiki squeal as he hurled himself after Var and raced from the Tower. He was free.

CHAPTER TWENTY-NINE

Maia found Yanna as she walked among the warriors who were driving sharpened stakes into the ground along the edge of the treeline. The arrow-ward was with her, handing newly fletched darts to the women sitting or lying on the travois behind the makeshift palisade. Unable to ride into battle, protected from charging wulfen and riders, their arrows would rain down on the battlefield and the enemy lines.

Maia could hear the sound of an axe, the chink of bridle decorations as the Eagle Hunters let their horses graze before leading them to their positions at each end of the line of stakes. The smell from the cooking fires and the growl of hunger in her stomach made her glad that they had decided to eat at sun-sleep. There were more fires than cooking pots. She had told them that Urteth must think that many warriors waited in the woods.

She looked from the slight rise where they camped, across the spread of the valley with its winding river and tall Tower and wondered if Urteth was watching their hasty preparations.

The last of the sun's rays tinged the grey stone with gold. It would be dark soon. Little time to make ready for what sun-wake would bring. Her band of warriors and hunters had arrived late. Their progress had been slow because the wounded rode with them.

Yanna followed her gaze. Saw an eagle flying to the Tower.

'At sun-sleep you could still send the killer to find Urteth,' she said.

Maia shook her head. To ask Var to kill Urteth would be so easy. So wrong. She knew he had watched her, waiting for her to make that request. She had started to avoid him so that she didn't weaken. She hadn't seen him since they had broken camp and ridden here.

'Tareth believes that Urteth will meet him and see that Elin must fail. That it's foolish to waste lives by fighting.'

Yanna huffed. 'We must rid ourselves of the Wulf Kin. Khandar will never be safe while they send raiding parties through the mountain passes. While Elin and Urteth lead them we'll never have peace.'

Maia sighed. Yanna was a warrior. Tareth was too, but he was also a weaver and had chosen to live in a cave above the sun-deeps with the peaceful Cliff Dwellers. To measure his life by the rhythms of the weed beds. He had tried to shield her from the demands of sun-fire and war. He would always try to keep the peace. She didn't trust Urteth. She feared Tareth would ride into a trap. She would ride with him when the sun rose to meet Urteth. She would embrace Sun Catcher destiny and use her fire to fight, to protect him.

Leaving Yanna and the arrow-ward to finish their patrol along the thin line of their troops, Maia went to find the man she called father.

He would not be persuaded. Would not argue with her. As darkness fell Maia had given in and they had sat and talked until the fires burned low and the archer guarding the camp suddenly called out.

'Someone comes. Horses!'

Maia grabbed her bow and rushed to the line of stakes. She could hear the faint sound of archers notching their arrows, the tightening of bowstrings. There was no other sound. She felt a surge of pride. She might be unworthy of their loyalty and courage, but she wouldn't fail them.

She slipped through the stakes, ran several paces down the incline, dropped on one knee and peered through the dark, her arrow ready to be released. Yanna knelt beside her.

'Two horses,' she whispered.

Not a full-scale attack. Perhaps a trick to draw them out from the woods.

'Don't skewer the horses. There's a stockade,' called a voice.

'How can you see in the dark?' demanded another.

A furry shape leapt past Maia, its tail flicking her face as it cleared her shoulder. It was a rat. She almost dropped her bow.

'Var?'

'And Kodo.'

He slid to the ground.

Maia hugged him. 'You escaped!'

'Var and Tiki helped. I've got the silk . . . Most of it.'

'How? What happened to you?'

Kodo took her arm, pulled her towards the gleam of the fire as Var silently followed with the two ponies. 'It's a long story.'

Tareth's shadow loomed. They heard his knife rasp home in its sheath. 'Then come to the fire and tell it.'

'Is there any food?' asked Kodo. 'I'm starving.'

No one else could eat and speak at the same time without choking, thought Maia, as Kodo dipped yet another flatbread into his steaming bowl and scooped up more food.

'Are you sure Elin and Caspia left the Tower?' she asked.

'We didn't see them pass,' said Tareth.

'They've gone to the Sun City,' said Kodo, his mouth full. 'Elin wants the stone.'

'How do you know all this?' demanded Tareth.

'I heard them. They said Altara was destroyed. That you were dead.' He couldn't meet Maia's eyes.

'But why did you go to the Tower? You were on the way to the city.'

'I met Caspia,' Kodo mumbled, looking down. 'With a Wulf Kin. I was taken to the Tower. Caspia, Elin and Urteth were there.'

'Caspia–' began Maia.

'When did Elin leave?' interrupted Tareth.

Even though Tareth was looking grim, Kodo was glad he had brushed aside the questions he saw springing to Maia's lips. 'Sun-wake. With a band of Wulf Kin. She has the story-coat and the sun-helmet.'

Tareth turned to Maia. 'If this is true, then Urteth has tricked us. He wants to delay us here while Elin takes the sun-stone. You must ride to the City, Maia. Protect the stone. Take Egon and the Eagle Hunters. And any archers Yanna can spare.'

'We should go together.'

'We cannot ride fast enough with the wounded. And if Urteth sees us leave, he will follow. Attack us in the mountain passes.'

'We can hold him here,' said Yanna. 'Give the Catcher a good start.'

Tareth nodded.

'We're too few to split our forces,' protested Maia.

'You must return to the city,' said Tareth. 'Azbarak will need your help to defeat Elin. She mustn't seize the stone. If the city is taken, you must hide the sun-stone.'

'I will,' said Maia. 'But not without you.'

Maia was aware that an archer with her hunting cat had moved to stand beside her on the rise. Yanna had insisted that she have a guard. Maia smiled at the girl and wondered if she looked as calm. She hoped so. She counted the number of Wulf Kin massed in front of the Tower. Those with eagles were in the centre. If Urteth attacked, he would launch these ranks first. Perhaps it was a mistake to place the hunters like two curved horns to protect the thin line of injured archers. She saw that Egon thought so as he sent several of his men with their eagles to wait among Yanna's archers.

Kodo was with them. She could see his dark head among the fox-fur hats of the Eagle Hunters. He had asked to ride with Huan. Var had taken himself off somewhere. She peered along the line, looking for the cheetah, Nefrar. He was with Yanna. Like everyone else, she was watching the two mounted figures who had come together on the open grassland between the Tower and the woods.

Maia crossed her thumbs and sent her thoughts winging towards Tareth as he rode towards the Tower, his eagle perched on his fist.

Tareth looked beyond the approaching rider whose eagle balanced on his shining fist. He could see the sun glinting on Wulf Kin mail. Some carried eagles and many who stood with their wulfen had round shields slung across their shoulders. These were not raiders from across the mountains – they stood like a fighting force. Urteth had trained an army of warriors.

He reined in his pony and waited for his brother. He was

shocked when he saw the stone-fire scars on Urteth's face and the bronze sheath he wore to cover his injured hand. He saw Urteth assess the damage to his leg.

'Greetings brother,' called Urteth. He gestured at KiKya. 'You have not lost your skill.'

'Nor you,' replied Tareth. 'That is a fine bird. Although it seems you have broken trust with our people. Since when did the Wulf Kin fly our eagles?'

Urteth rode closer. 'What does a weaver who stole the sun-stone and fled from Khandar know of life in these mountains? The Eagle People are not alone in their love for eagles. The Wulf Kin hunt here too.'

'I've seen their hunting,' said Tareth. 'I come from Altara.'

Urteth shrugged. 'The archers betrayed Elin,' he said.

'When did one of the royal family of Khandar allow the Wulf Kin the freedom to destroy her people?'

'Much has changed since you stole the stone and the child, brother.'

'So it seems,' agreed Tareth grimly. 'You were the Queen's warrior then. Have the Wulf Kin replaced you, brother?'

A tide of red stained Urteth's face. 'I am Elin's consort. Our daughter Caspia is to be Queen after Elin.'

'Queen of this valley perhaps. Of this tainted Tower, of the Wulf Kin you have allowed to leave their wastelands. Not Queen of Khandar. Elin has lost that right. Her sister Maia is Sun Catcher and rules in the Sun City.'

'She is queen of nothing,' sneered Urteth. 'Without silk, without gold, without the stone. Elin has all. Your Sun Catcher has nothing.' He pointed at the group on the rise. 'Just a puny army that cannot stand against my Wulf Kin. A few birds to challenge our eagles. Wounded archers. The usurper will be defeated before sun-high. Surrender brother. I will be merciful.'

'Using the same mercy Elin showed her sisters when she killed them so that she could rule alone?' scorned Tareth.

Urteth glowered, anger turning his scars purple. 'An old tale. A lie. The plague and fire killed them.'

'Elin was the plague. And your Wulf Kin set the fire.'

'I will spare you, brother. Let you slink aboard a ship and flee from the Queen's revenge and my Wulf Kin. Set your eagle free, ride as far and as fast as you can, and I will let you go.'

Tareth laughed. 'But I will not spare you. Nor will the Warriors. Nor the Sun Catcher.'

Urteth glared at his brother. 'Send me the girl,' he demanded. 'She's of little use to you if she doesn't hold the sun-stone.' He touched his scarred face with his bronze wrist guard. 'You shouldn't have left the city and the stone unguarded, brother. Send her to me and I will let the Eagle People return to their homes. I have no quarrel with them.'

'You have enslaved their eagles, Urteth. They have come to free them. They won't allow you, or the Wulf Kin who follow you, to remain here in their mountains. They will fight.'

'Then they will die, and you with them, brother!' snarled Urteth. He cast his eagle.

The Weaver's pony reared. KiKya screamed and launched herself at her rival. The eagles struck, fought and plummeted to the ground. Before Tareth could control his mount and free his knife, Urteth had notched an arrow to his bow. As Tareth forced the horse down, turning to come to the aid of his eagle, his brother let fly. The Weaver lurched in the saddle. The pony wheeled and ran back across the valley, its rider clinging to its mane.

CHAPTER THIRTY

Maia watched the desperate flight of Tareth's pony. Egon raced to meet it. Riding beside it, he guided the stampeding pony towards the stockade. Maia waited as Huan caught Tareth. She wanted to run to see if he was badly hurt, but saw Urteth raise his arm, heard the drumming of knife hilts on metal as the Wulf Kin massed at the foot of the Tower started to surge towards their leader and the two eagles that still fought at his horses' feet. Yanna was calling to the archers. She could hear the singing cry of the Eagle Hunters.

Everything seemed to slow down. KiKya broke free and flew clumsily towards the rise. Maia watched Urteth take aim. She saw KiKya tumble and her slayer raise his fist. Sunlight glinted on his bronze hand, shone on the shield slung on his saddle.

Behind her the archers were reaching for their arrows, releasing the braids on their bows. As the plaits shivered, the silk thread sang. Then her world narrowed to the figure of the horseman in the black wolf-pelt who had shot Tareth and killed his eagle.

Fury raged through her. She began to burn, pain and heat licked at her, her eyes wept fire. She couldn't see through the raging flames. She raised her hands. Molten gold ran through her fingers as she gathered the sunlight, pulling it towards her, dragging it deep inside her where it churned and boiled. Urteth would die for his treachery.

'Maia! Don't!' Tareth's voice called.

'No!' yelled Var.

'Stop!' Kodo shrieked.

She knew they were sprinting towards her.

It was too late. She couldn't hold back. Couldn't breathe. The pain would split her in two. She had to stop Urteth. Had to end the Wulf Kin. Had to save the warriors and the hunters before the half-wild beasts reached them. She was fire. She was flame. Light spat from her fingers.

Urteth yelled. Raised his shield. The shaft of flame struck the burnished surface, shattered, and splinters of fire spun around the buckler and streamed back towards Maia. Fractured shafts of light spilled onto the shields of the Wulf Kin close to him as they locked their shields in a bright wall that reflected the brilliant darts and flung them at the stockade and the figure of flames standing between them and the archers.

Var shouted again.

Maia felt the change in the light, a hot rushing wind and

streamers of heat streaking towards her. She heard a flight of arrows. Felt them burst into flame.

'Sun Catcher!' bellowed Egon.

Someone screamed.

She flung out her arms and was knocked to the ground.

'No!'

Var sprinted towards her. Strands of light coiled like snakes around her. She raised her hands. Sunlight streamed from them.

'No. No.'

Var saw the Wulf Kin lift their shields. He heard the clash of metal as they crashed together in a shining wall.

He was too slow. He'd never reach her. He saw Kodo sprinting. Heard the thunder of pony hooves as Egon charged towards the shimmering figure.

Shafts of gold crackled above him as Maia flung fire. He heard Kodo shout as he hurled himself in front of Maia as the bolt of light hit the burnished shields. He saw Maia turn, throw up her arms to try to deflect the blow as sunfire bounced from the gleaming shields. The warrior beside her staggered. Her bow braid caught fire. He was blinded by the blaze. He was too late to save her.

Var leapt. The Wulf Kin's roar was the sound of storm winds bellowing through mountain passes. He was tossed into a rolling wave of molten gold. Battered by the blast of heat, he tumbled towards the howling darkness that swallowed him.

Var moved. He managed to open his eyes.

They were losing. The eagles were outnumbered. He saw the Eagle Hunters charging towards the fighting birds as they tumbled from the sky locked in a mortal struggle with Urteth's eagles. He heard the wulfen bay as they were released to attack the hunters.

Maia was curled on the ground, fists clenched, eyes closed. Kodo lay stunned beside her.

'Don't die, don't die,' Var muttered as he crawled towards her. The drumming of shields and the roar of the Wulf Kin seemed to recede as waves of weakness washed over him. He collapsed and lay still listening to his harsh breathing. The ground beneath his cheek trembled. They must be crashing their spears onto the ground, driving themselves and their beasts into a frenzy as they prepared to charge.

Maia was as still as stone.

He had to reach her.

He could see figures swaying, locked in battle. The archers still fought to protect Maia from Urteth's Wulf Kin as they surged across the valley. The Sun Catcher had tried to save them. He'd been too late to knock her aside. Too late to save the warrior guarding her.

He must get up. His skin stung. Black spots floated in his eyes. Var rubbed them, trying to clear his vision. Beneath his fingers his skin felt tight, his hair scorched and ragged as feathers. He felt as hollow and light as a bird. He wondered if he was dying. He thought he could hear crows calling. Heard the chink of stone striking against stone. He knew he had something still to do. Hands like claws seemed to lift him, drag him onto his knees.

He groaned. The Watcher had told him to protect the Sun Catcher. He had failed. He must recover her body. He forced himself to move, his gaze fixed on the crumpled shape sprawled on the ground.

'Don't die.' He wasn't sure if he was begging Maia or himself to banish the shadows waiting to smother him.

He thought he saw her move. But it was only the eagle feather in her hair stirring in the wind.

The branches above him swayed as a sudden gust breathed across the valley. Clouds were gathering. As he watched the storm swallowing the blue sky, he knew that the darkness would blot out the sun. It was the end of hope. The Sun Catcher was dead.

'Maia,' he croaked.

The crows replied.

He looked up. The trees were black with roosting birds. He could feel their beady eyes watching him. They would tumble down and scavenge across the trampled grasslands once the fighting was over. They would peck out the eyes of the dead. He shuddered. A single bird fell from the trees as if jostled from its perch by the others. It landed near Maia. Another joined it. They fluttered closer.

'Leave her alone!'

Var struggled to his feet, his hands reaching inside his tunic.

214

Maia coughed. One crow tugged at her hair. The other pecked her hand.

Kodo moaned and tried to sit up.

Var's hand curled round a stone. He felt the runes wriggling across his skin.

He knew what he must do. He hurled the black stone with all his strength at the crows.

'I choose, Watcher!' he yelled. 'I choose!'

His hand shook. His aim was poor. The stone flew upwards, hit a tree, ricocheted and exploded into a myriad of black shards that shot into the crowd of crows roosting high in the branches. They rose in a shrieking mass. Var thought he saw each spinning splinter sprout feathers, grow beaks, claws.

The flock of real and stone crows wheeled above him in a huge, ever-widening spiral climbing towards the dark clouds. Var saw the whirling mass torn apart by the winds blustering and bellowing beneath the thunder tower, the birds tossed like leaves as they were sucked into the darkness and vanished.

'Var?' Maia wobbled to her feet. Var grabbed her. She gazed over the battlefield.

'I failed,' she gasped. 'We've lost.'

'Not yet,' said Var. 'Wait.'

The roaring wind hit them, almost knocking them down again. They clung to each other. The trees bowed beneath the blast. Branches crashed to the ground. Above their heads the clouds split. And arrowing across the battlefield, mobbing eagles, smothering Urteth, falling on wulfen, attacking Wulf Kin came black, tumbling waves of red-legged crows.

215

CHAPTER THIRTY-ONE

The silver gates swung slowly open. Azbarak stood waiting, his skin gleaming with scented oil. As he raised his hands, his silver rings shone and perfume wafted from his coat.

Caspia knew she smelled of horse and dust.

'Welcome, my Queen. Greetings, Lady Caspia.'

Elin's voice was sharp. 'You kept us waiting at the gates.'

'I will punish the gatekeeper,' promised Azbarak. 'It is good to see you again.'

'Was it good to serve the Sun Catcher?'

'I serve the city,' said Azbarak. 'As I always do.'

'You serve yourself, Keeper. As you always do. You will be wise to remember where your loyalty lies.'

'Yes, my Queen.'

Elin scowled at him. 'Altara was not loyal. The archers are

dead. You will have to find a new royal guard. The Weaver and his daughter, the so-called Sun Catcher, are no more. Caspia, the future Queen, will claim the stone, and catch the sun.'

Azbarak allowed his expression to soften. 'Then I will serve her as I have served you. Do you expect Urteth soon? I will need to prepare for the celebrations.'

He smiled at Caspia. 'I will summon jugglers, acrobats, performers to entertain you. The harvest has been good. There will be plenty for the feast.' He looked at Elin. 'Traders returned to the city once the rivers were free of ice. The people are content. They will be pleased that you are here. '

Elin's eyes narrowed. 'They followed the usurper.'

'She found the stone. But she has deserted them. The city will welcome their queens.' He inclined his head. 'Mother and daughter.'

Elin kneed her pony forward. Azbarak stepped swiftly aside. Caspia noticed the flicker of anger in his eyes. She probed his thoughts but found nothing. It was a game they had played since she could remember. A game Azbarak always used to let her win when she was small. She realised that he'd kept his thoughts hidden from her for many star-shifts.

'Welcome home, Lady Caspia,' he smiled.

'My mother has the story-coat and the sun-helmet,' she said. 'I will wear them at solstice when I catch the sun.'

Azbarak nodded. 'They will be kept safe until then.'

Maia pushed Nefrar's nose away. She couldn't bear to be touched. She felt as if her skin was peeling off. To make it worse, she itched. She would go mad if the itching didn't stop. The cheetah huffed his disapproval and padded away.

She ought to be glad that the battle was over, that Tareth lived and most of the archers and hunters had survived. Those who had stood close to her and had been splashed by flecks of her fire bore scatterings of tiny red marks where they had been burned. They called them Sun Catcher stars, displaying them with pride. The stockade looked as if it was covered with dappled horse hide. It could have been so much worse, she thought, and tried not to consider how Urteth had tricked her with his wall of shields and nearly destroyed her. Urteth was dead, his Wulf Kin army scattered.

She wriggled, trying to stop her tunic chaffing. She wished she could shed her skin like the green snakes that slid among the sweet-smelling gorse bushes on the cliffs above the sun-deeps. She rubbed her eyes. The eye-bright the healer had smeared across them had cleared the smoke which dimmed her vision. Perhaps this time she had shut the lids against the worst of the blazing light.

The healer crouched beside her holding a bowl of crushed heal-leaf.

She touched Maia's hand and transparent flakes that gleamed like pearls covered her fingertips.

Fish scales, thought Maia. I'm turning into a fish. She felt the flakes crumble, become dust. Not skin. Silk. Her silent silk had been crisped by the fire. It had saved her. She remembered the voice as the light had cocooned her. The silk had called her name. Beneath the dry scales her skin was untouched.

The healer pressed her forefinger against Maia's cheekbone. The stinging eased.

She beckoned to Var who was muttering over his knives. She took his hand. The back was dusted with angry red marks. The healer scooped heal-leaf paste onto her palm, stirred in the dust from her fingers and smoothed it over Var's hand. The red burns faded, leaving only tiny white scars.

'A sun-fire balm,' smiled the healer. She started brushing the silk dust and scales from Maia's skin into the dish of heal-leaf as she called for her helpers to bring empty bowls and wisps of pony tail.

Maia lay still when the healer had gone. Her skin felt as if it had been polished. Tareth stared at the bowl of silk dust at Maia's side. He stirred it with his finger.

'No whispers?'

Maia shook her head. 'It never sang. I thought it must be because it was woven by the sun-deeps. Because it had no stories to sing.'

'There were stories in the weed beds,' said Tareth.

'Perhaps it knew I was afraid of it.'

'It's good to be afraid. The silk can be dangerous.'

'But it always brought me comfort,' said Maia. 'And it helped to mend KiKya's injuries. Perhaps its purpose was to heal. To be burned and become balm for a catcher's fire.' She touched her cheek. The skin was cool and smooth. 'I must ask the healer to mix it with heal-leaf.'

'So that it brings comfort and healing to those touched by sun-fire.' He smiled at her. 'Kodo showed me his scar.

He's as proud of it as he is of his tattooed thumb.' He shifted uncomfortably, trying to ease his wounded shoulder. 'He told me what happened in the desert and when he left you to carry the moth eggs and cocoons to the city.' He touched the back-sack which lay beside him. 'I owe him much. He saved the silk. I can start a new garden and teach Zena to weave the silk and care for the moon-moths. Together we'll make more silk. For you and Kodo.'

Maia wasn't surprised. Zena was too gentle to take joy in fighting. She would be a fine weaver if she were strong enough not to succumb to silk dreams. She remembered how Zena had followed her from Altara carrying the story-coat. She hadn't heard its song. The silk would not enslave Zena.

'Silk for Kodo?' she asked.

Tareth nodded. 'You were right. You must take Kodo with you to the Sun City. Let him wear Xania's coat. He told me what the silk had shown him.'

He closed his eyes and fell silent for so long that Maia thought that the sleep-drink from the healer had worked. She left his hand resting on the back-sack and smoothed his sleeping fur around his shoulders.

'The coat will choose the singer,' he muttered drowsily. 'Kodo will be your Story Singer.'

Maia nudged Kodo. His face was bright with stories as he carefully folded the fragile strips of silk and tucked them in his belt pouch. He was happy. Maia had convinced him that he was Xania's successor. Tareth had told him to hold the silk, to listen to its stories. He had given Kodo all but one of the strips that had hung in the moth-garden. He had kept only the silk which sang Xania's story.

Kodo's fingers caressed the silk. It was an effort to close the pouch and let the old silk rest. It had so much to share. He heard it whisper.

'Soon,' he reassured it. 'I'll find you again soon.'

'Does it still sing?' asked Maia.

'Sometimes,' said Kodo. 'But it's old and the whispers are faint. I think it listens more. I tell it what I can see. It took the song of the Eagle Hunters and the story of the crows. I'll never forget that sight.'

Var looked up. 'The Watcher summoned them. With her stone.' He touched the white stone which remained inside his tunic.

'She did that with bees once,' said Kodo. 'D'you think she made the Storm Chaser send the storm clouds that brought the birds?'

Maia shook her head.

'I think she did,' said Kodo.

'When you go back to the Stilt Village, you must ask her,' said Maia.

The last of the silk dreams faded from his eyes. 'I'm the Story Singer. I must stay.'

Maia had been thoughtless. Kodo had always dreamed of becoming a trader. The silk had chosen him. The silk hated water. But the silent silk that Tareth had woven for her in the Cliff Village had survived her journey on Trader Bron's boat.

Perhaps the new silk was different.

'There are stories beyond the mountains and the Vast,' she said. 'You will have to sing those stories too.'

Kodo grinned. 'Perhaps I'll sing them for Ootey and the Storm Chaser,' he said.

'Yes,' said Maia. 'You have to tell Razek's story.'

Kodo rolled his eyes. 'Which he'll never tire of hearing. Doesn't the Singer choose which tale to sing?'

'Ask the silk,' suggested Maia.

'I can now, can't I,' Kodo grinned at her. 'No more secrets.'

'No,' said Maia.

'Good,' said Kodo. He leapt onto his pony and chased after Huan, who was riding far out on the sword-hand side of their small group while his eagle hunted low across the grasslands.

Maia watched Nefrar racing to join them, with Yanna in close pursuit. They were all in good spirits. She was glad they had put the memory of the battle behind them.

She wished she could feel as free as they seemed. She should be happy that Urteth was defeated. She had found the Story Singer. Tareth had the silk and was following slowly with the injured. Before the snows of wolf-walk he would have made a new moth-garden. She must take the waning sun-stone from the Catching stone, then keep it safe in the Sun Palace until it was time for the sun to be caught again and the land warmed.

She touched the fire scar on her cheek. Her friends had forgotten what still needed to be done. She could not. She was the Sun Catcher. She must find the power to overcome Elin – and Caspia.

CHAPTER THIRTY-TWO

The Sun Palace was quiet. Caspia was restless. She wished her father would come. Urteth would fill the rooms with noise and action. Elin's silence was unnerving. Even the Wulf Kin avoided the solar where Elin sat and waited for messages from the Tower of Eagles.

She'd hardly seen Vultek or his wulfen since they arrived in the city. Perhaps she would send for him and go hunting beyond the city. A city that, despite preparations for solstice, seemed subdued. She no longer went there. Few met her eyes. Some flicked their fingers in greeting and then glanced from her to the stone that still gleamed high above the Stone Court.

She wondered if Azbarak had been too glib in his assurance that the Sun City welcomed their return. He was the only one who could rouse her mother from her thoughts when he consulted her about the decisions to be made for taking the dimming crystal from the catching stone. She wasn't prepared to wait. Once Urteth came, they would expect her to wear the story-coat and the sun-helmet and she would rule alongside her mother.

Caspia heard the sound of someone arriving and Azbarak's bellow of welcome and rushed to the window. She was disappointed. It wasn't Urteth. Below in the courtyard a troupe of young boys and girls were tumbling from a cart. A slender girl with a long, dark plait rounded them up like a mother hen and shepherded them into the palace. Taller children clambered out of the cart, carrying furled banners, a monkey, bulging bags from which spilled brightly coloured clothes. One boy dropped a set of copper discs which rolled, clanging, across the stones. Greeting Azbarak, retrieving their dropped goods, they followed the tall girl.

Caspia felt her spirits lift. They must be the jugglers and acrobats Azbarak had promised to find. She would tell the Keeper to bring them to the solar to entertain them. Perhaps they would amuse Elin. Anything would be better than this silent vigil in the cold Sun Palace.

Maia approached the Sun City under the cover of dark. The main gates were closed.

Var led them to a small postern and made them wait beneath the walls.

224

'I will open the gate.'

He scrambled onto Huan's pony, used the boy's back to climb higher and, picking out hand- and footholds, scaled the wall.

'Like a lizard,' whispered Kodo as Var disappeared.

The wooden gate creaked open. Var beckoned.

'The way is clear,' he hissed. 'I will find Azbarak. He will open the palace gates for you.'

Maia felt for her shoulder sheath, and the warm bone handle of the knife Tareth had given her as she left the Tower comforted her. Tareth wouldn't hesitate to take Elin's life. She mustn't weaken. She felt Kodo's pony nudge hers. His eyes were bright with excitement. Maia drew in a deep breath.

They rode into the city and through the narrow, climbing streets towards the Sun Palace.

Caspia watched the acrobats spinning across the floor. They flipped hand over hand towards Azbarak to form a wall. It grew into a pyramid, towering higher as more children were lifted and swung up to stand on the shoulders of those below. A tall girl, her long plait swinging, scaled the tower, a scarlet flame in baggy tunic and trousers. She reached the top and found her balance. A boy on the bottom row called, the wall collapsed and the girl dived to the floor among the tumbling acrobats. She landed like a cat. As she bowed and ran off with the acrobats, two girls throwing spinning copper discs to each other ran towards the dais.

Azbarak, lifting his gold cup, drummed his feet so hard on the dais that it made Caspia's seat tremble, and bellowed his approval. The acrobats in their gaudy clothes streamed back, clustering like moths around the jugglers. Two boys in black followed them, twirling banners above their heads. A third striding between them juggled red leather balls. Caspia could hear them slapping against his palms. The balls flew faster and faster.

Caspia clapped her hands, enjoying the confusion. She saw Azbarak brushing beads of liquid from his coat as he slipped from the solar. The dark juggler stepped forward to join Azbarak.

Caspia glanced at her mother, resting her head on her hand as she watched the leaping children. Elin hadn't noticed Azbarak's departure. Caspia rose. The tall, dark girl in scarlet grabbed her so that the smallest children could tumble underneath their joined hands. The children danced around her and tugged at Caspia's gown, encouraging her to spin with them. The girl met her eyes.

Caspia caught a stray thought. She dropped the girl's hand, twitched her skirt free of the tiny, grasping hands, and followed Azbarak.

The silver gates opened. Maia led the way. Azbarak, shivering in the cold air beckoned them to follow. The ponies' muffled hooves made little noise as they rode across the courtyard. Leaving their mounts with an archer, they climbed the steps into the palace and hurried along a corridor towards the dead moth-garden. The hairs on the back of Var's neck pricked.

When he had last entered the Sun Palace, he had come to kill the Sun Catcher. The branch of a thorn bush snagged his tunic. The spikes grazed his skin as he pulled himself free. It was here that he had been attacked by the Weaver and his eagle. Here that Azbarak had hit him with a lamp. He hoped the Keeper was not leading them into a trap. The man seemed nervous, his eyes searching the shadows as he hurried through the palace. Var could smell his sweat beneath the waft of perfumed oil. He could hear the wheeze of Azbarak's breath. He eased himself between Maia and the Keeper.

The large man led the way into a room to one side of the garden. There was hardly space for all of them. Azbarak squeezed his bulk through the door, leaving it ajar.

'I must return to the solar before I am missed,' he whispered. He counted heads. 'Is this all the support you bring, Sun Catcher?'

'Do I need more, Keeper?' demanded Maia. 'I have come to claim the sun-stone, not to fight.'

Azbarak shrugged. 'You are not the only claimant, Catcher. Others wait to release the stone.'

'So who do you serve?'

'I serve the Sun City,' said Azbarak. 'Who else follows? Urteth? Wulf Kin?'

'Urteth is dead.'

There was a gasp. The door was pushed wide and a tall

girl in red, her arm around Caspia's neck, fell into the room. Caspia screeched, her nails raking at the girl's arm.

'She was listening.'

Caspia squirmed. A knife glinted in her hand. She lashed out at Maia.

Kodo slammed his fist down onto her wrist. The knife clattered to the ground.

Caspia glared at Kodo her eyes brilliant with tears. 'I thought you were my friend, silk-thief.'

Kodo picked up the knife and stuck it in his belt. 'Trader and lizard boy.' He straightened. 'And Story Singer.'

Caspia laughed. 'Not without the story-coat.'

Her gaze shifted to Azbarak. 'How did they get into the palace? Call the Wulf Kin. Release me!'

Azbarak nodded. The girl loosened her grip.

Caspia rubbed her throat. Her ring glowed red. 'You have walked into another trap, usurper. You cannot escape. Azbarak serves me! As do the Wulf Kin.' She glared at Azbarak. 'Call them. Take her to Elin.'

Azbarak shrugged. 'There are no Wulf Kin in the palace to serve you.'

'You lie!' said Caspia. 'My father sent Wulf Kin to escort us.'

Ruby sparks swirled in her ring. A bead of light appeared on its surface. Fell to the floor. It sizzled and rolled towards Azbarak's shoe.

'Summon Vultek!' she screamed.

Yanna thumped her bow on the glowing bead as if it were a poisonous spider scuttling across the floor. The bead split, shedding tiny balls that raced across the floor. Maia felt as if she had stepped on a spine-back as a fragment bounced onto her foot. She shook it off, remembering how Elin's jewel had spat blue sparks. She saw the others jumping to avoid the spinning glimmers.

Yanna flicked a ball of light across the small room. It hit the wall, hissed and died.

'A child's trick,' she jeered.

'My father will come.' The light in her gemstone died. Caspia clenched her fists. 'He will punish you all.'

Maia shook her head. 'Urteth was killed at the Tower of Eagles.' She felt Caspia steal the truth from the minds of the others.

'It isn't true. My father promised to come. You are trying to trick me. Vultek, come to me!' she shrieked as she fled from the room.

Var leapt after her.

Azbarak sighed. 'She will not find the Wulf Kin. Var will catch her.' He turned to Maia. 'I couldn't tell her that her father was dead. Nor carry such tidings to Elin.'

His voice was smooth, his face bland. Maia wondered if it was fear of Elin's rage and grief when he told her of Urteth's fate that had kept him silent, or sympathy for Caspia, who had loved her father.

'No Wulf Kin in the palace?'

Azbarak shook his head.

'Or in the city?' Maia wondered if that was why they had slipped undetected through the passageways to the palace.

'Zartev, Urteth's champion, left the city before sun-wake. He rode towards the mountains. The rest . . .' he spread his hands wide.

'The urchin army,' said Yanna. 'A troupe of killers.'

Azbarak smiled. 'Loyal children who have many skills.'

Maia felt a flicker of anger. 'And are you loyal?' she demanded fiercely. 'Do you serve my father and me?'

'I have served the city and awaited your return.'

'And the return of Elin,' spat Yanna.

Azbarak's expression didn't change. 'Tareth commanded me to protect the city. To do what I must, what I thought best.'

'It is best to follow the Catcher!' growled Yanna.

'She left the city,' said Azbarak. 'She is young.'

'I have returned,' said Maia. 'To hold the stone as a Sun Catcher must. And while it sleeps through wolf-walk, I will restore the moth-garden with Tareth.'

'Elin claims that Caspia will take and hold the stone. The Queen waits in the solar. Caspia will join her,' Azbarak told Maia. 'If you are the true Catcher, you must challenge their claim to the throne.'

Maia looked him squarely in the face.

'That is why I am here,' she said.

CHAPTER THIRTY-THREE

Maia tugged off her boots. The stone beneath her feet was still warm. It would be easier to scale the cairn with bare feet. She wondered if the sun-stone heated the smooth rocks. If it did, would her feet and hands blister before she reached the crystal?

Caspia was standing barefoot next to her mother. She must think that the waning power of the sun-stone meant that the cairn would be cool. Elin would have told her. Elin and her sisters would have watched their Sun Catcher mother retrieve the stone each leaf-fall.

Maia realised how little she knew of the traditions of Khandar. She sighed. At least the climb would be easier than the scramble to harvest gull eggs or to take honey from the bee cleft.

Kodo was watching Caspia. 'She looks like you. She liked

lizards, she knew that I wanted silk. She seemed kinder than you.'

Maia tried not to let her hurt show.

'I thought that you didn't trust me. That you believed in Razek and Var more,' confessed Kodo. 'So I listened to what Caspia said. I didn't think you thought I was worthy to listen to the silk stories.'

'The silk was Tareth's secret,' said Maia. 'He knew it was dangerous to others. It belonged to my family. And you stole it,' she added. 'Why should I have trusted you?'

Kodo thought. 'Because you were my friend?' he suggested.

Maia laughed.

Azbarak frowned. The solemnity of the occasion did not allow for mirth. Once again he felt his loyalties waver. This Catcher was too young. Ignorant of her duties. She hadn't grown up in the Sun Palace like Caspia.

'Are you regretting your weakness, Keeper?' sneered Elin. 'You shouldn't have allowed her to live. See how she laughs at you and the city you serve. Caspia will be Catcher. You know this.'

'The stone will decide who will reign ,' replied Azbarak.

'I am the Queen. I decide. And my daughter will rule after me.'

'Then I shall serve her well, as I have ever done for your family, if the sun-stone wills it.'

'If she'll have you,' countered Elin. 'The city nearly knew famine under your care.'

Azbarak studied the cuffs of his embroidered coat and bit back the temptation to remind Elin that her rule had known the loss of the sun-stone, the lengthening of wolf-walk, poor harvests and cold new-leaf. Maia had delivered the sun-stone and caught the sun.

'The sun-catch brought a good harvest. The granaries are full.' He was satisfied as an angry flush rose on Elin's cheeks.

'Keeper,' Caspia's voice was cool. It carried across the courtyard. 'When I have the stone, you will seize the usurper, and execute her. She has killed my father. She tried to steal my mother's throne.'

'And if you do not Keeper, then my assassin will,' said Elin. She looked at Var. 'He failed to kill the girl once. He will not fail again.'

Var moved to stand behind the red witch. He looked at Maia and wondered if she understood the message in his eyes. Then he gazed up at the waning gleam of the sun-stone and closed his mind to everything. He was a Death Bringer. He did not choose. Azbarak had chosen for him when he was wandering lost in the Hidden. The Keeper always chose. He rocked onto the balls of his feet and felt the knife sheath flex in his boot.

Maia's laughter stuck in her throat. She leaned towards Kodo.

'If I fail, you must take the story-coat and flee,' she murmured.

Kodo shook his head. 'You won't fail.'

'I don't intend to,' said Maia. 'But you must make Azbarak take you to the storerooms and find the coat. You have to keep the stories safe. You are the Story Singer. If the Keeper cannot assist you, Tiki can discover where Elin has taken it and Var will help you leave the city safely.'

'Var!' said Kodo. 'He has betrayed you.'

'He summoned the Watcher's crows. Saved us from defeat. I trust him.'

'He's a killer.'

'He's a friend,' said Maia. 'As you are.'

She walked across the courtyard to Caspia. The girl's face was pale but two red spots burned on her cheeks.

'You don't have to do this,' she said. 'The sun-stone is my . . . burden.'

Caspia glared at her, her lips thinned. 'It is no burden. It's my birthright. I am the Queen's daughter. You are the last and the least of her sisters. You cannot rule.'

'I am the Sun Catcher,' said Maia. 'You do not have to attempt to hold the stone.' Maia tried not to think of what had happened to Caspia's father when he had reached out to catch it.

Caspia caught the half-stifled memory. Her eyes flashed. 'You will not trick me as you did my father. You will not weaken me as you are weak. I want what is mine by right.'

Maia felt a stab of admiration. She couldn't fault Caspia's courage.

'Then let the sun-stone decide,' she said, and walked around the cairn until it stood between herself and Caspia. She drew in a deep breath and fixed her eyes on the sun-stone. From the corner of her eye she saw Azbarak lift his hand.

'Let the stone choose,' he boomed.

No booming waves crashed against the red cliffs, no gangs of gulls dived at her head, no wind tugged her from her handholds. It wasn't like the cliffs at all. The stones were hot beneath her toes. Maia heard Caspia gasp as if the heat was greater than it was. The rocks were smooth, like huge sea-smoothed pebbles edging the weed bed levees.

She leaned away from the sheer rockface, gripping with her toes, looking for the easiest way to the stone in its niche at the top of the cairn. The sky above was streaked with pink and gold. A shaft of sunlight pierced the hidden stone like a gold blade. Light fell over her upturned face, trickled over her shoulders, running into her, cool yet warm. The sun-stone was calling her. Maia felt sunlight fizz inside her. Tucking one leg beneath her, stretching the other for balance she reached up and looked at the stone column with its hole like the eye of a needle. The spear of sunlight pierced her. She cried out. Her eyes burned gold with molten fire.

She flung out her hand to block the sun. Tentacles of light curled round her fingers. Threads of gold wrapped her like the silk Tareth teased from the cocoons. She was bound in a shroud of gleaming gossamer, fragile as moon-moth wings, strong as stone, bright as a burnished shield.

She lifted her arms. They were wings. She was dressed in sunlight, her cloak of fire streaming in the wind.

'Sun Catcher!' yelled Kodo.

Caspia screamed and slid from the cairn, trailing wisps of smoke.

Cruel hands pulled her to her feet, hurled her against the cairn.

'Climb girl, climb!' shrieked Elin. 'She is sun-mazed! Quickly! She hasn't taken the stone. Move.'

Caspia sobbed. It hurt. Her hands were on fire. She tried to grasp the smooth rock. Tried to find a finger-hold that didn't scorch her skin. Her thoughts were smoke and heat.

'I can't.'

Elin pushed her aside and started to climb, scaling the cairn like a winged beetle scuttling from stone to hot stone.

Maia heard the song of the sun. High, fierce, liquid, surging with flame and ringing like ice struck with a spear. She was swimming between waving fronds of gold-tinged kelp, towed deeper and deeper towards the sun disc. Bubbles steamed from her mouth, her nose, her ears. She was drowning in the sun-deeps. She was the sun.

Maia lifted the sun-stone from its niche. She held it up to the sun, cradled it as she would a baby.

Elin screamed. 'Kill her!'

Var slipped his knife from his boot. Twisted it in his hand, watching it turn black then silver as blade and handle were lit by the rays of the sun. He stood poised, the tip in his fingers, the knife shoulder high.

'Var! No!' shouted Kodo, running towards him.

'I choose, red witch,' called Var.

He raised his heart hand, and hurled the Watcher's white pebble towards the golden figure kneeling at the top of the cairn. It clipped the top stone close to Maia and clattered down the side.

Elin cried as a huge white gull, its wingspan as wide as a sea-eagle's, glided past her. She ducked to avoid it and slipped. As she looked up she was struck by a shaft of sunlight and lost her grip. She plunged from the cairn and hit the ground at Var's feet.

Var looked down at the bundle of broken bones and cloth. He brushed back the hem of Elin's skirt and picked up the white stone.

'I choose,' he said. 'But not you, witch.'

CHAPTER THIRTY-FOUR

'Elin is dead.'

Maia placed the sun-stone in the woven hazel nest Tareth had made. She brushed away the strands of light that clung to it. They drifted onto the slender twigs, burnishing them with gold.

The sun-stone no longer gleamed. It was a dull grey lump. She touched it like a mother touching the cheek of a sleeping infant. She wondered if far in the mountains the crystals in the cave beyond the sunken lake were singing. The stone lay silent. It would sleep throughout the dark of wolf-walk while she watched over it, keeping it safe until the next solstice. She blinked, trying to shift the jagged dark which seemed to rim her eyes. She felt spent, hollow. She wished she could sleep like the stone and forget the sound of Elin's body hitting the flagstones.

Kodo thought he saw the traces of light still hovering round Maia.

'Killed by Var,' he said, his voice hoarse.

'By a bird,' said Yanna.

'By the Watcher's stone,' croaked Kodo. He shivered. The old crone and her crows had always spooked him. She knew too much.

'The fall killed her,' said Egon.

'It was the sun-stone,' said Azbarak. 'And the Catcher.'

Var said nothing.

'She's dead, which is all that matters,' concluded Yanna.

Maia rose to her feet. 'And Caspia?'

'Alive. A healer is with her. Her hands are blistered,' said Egon.

Maia glanced at her own palms. Scratched, grubby, but unburned. 'Were the stones so hot?'

'They glowed as you climbed,' said Kodo.

'Did we bring silk-heal with us?' Maia asked Yanna.

The warrior nodded.

'Then we must send some to the healer for Caspia's hands and feet.'

Yanna nodded and left. Nefrar nudged Maia with his nose and padded after the warrior.

Azbarak crossed to her, holding her boots as if they were a precious trophy.

'Command me, Sun Catcher.'

Maia's grip tightened round the sun-stone nest. She quailed at the decisions she must make. Kodo and Var stood close. They were careful to avoid the light drifting from the stone.

'There is much for you to do, Keeper,' she said.

She glanced at the bundle of cloth huddled at the foot of the cairn. It looked like a fallen bird, not Elin's body. She was glad of that.

'Elin must be buried. Her sisters lie on the Cloud Plains.'

Maia remembered flags blowing at the corners of a heavy cart, snow carried on the bitter wind, the wailing dirge of silk as Xania was placed beneath the log roof and stones of the forever cairn.

'Elin shall lie with Urteth close to the Tower of Eagles,' she decided.

Azbarak nodded. 'It shall be done.'

'I expect Caspia will wish to accompany her mother,' said Maia. 'Yanna and the Warrior Women will ride with her.'

Maia gazed at the sun-stone. She wondered if she dared set Caspia free.

'The sun-stone . . .' She had forgotten what she had to do. She stifled a yawn.

Azbarak came to her rescue. 'It is custom for the Sun Catcher to show the stone to the people of the city. Your mother would walk through the streets, carrying the stone, before she placed it in the palace to sleep before the next solstice.'

Maia sighed. A sleeping stone and an empty palace. She would be alone. No family of seven sisters chattered in the echoing rooms. Her friends would leave. Yanna said Azbarak had brought children to the city. She would fill the Sun Palace with their light and laughter and life. And stories. There had been too much sadness.

She was a new Sun Catcher. She had found a Story Singer. It was a beginning.

Caspia dismissed the healer and told her to send warm chay and food. The woman ignored her, finished tidying her potions and wrappings before she left, closing the door. Caspia scowled. At least the woman had known how to take the pain away from her hands and feet. The cool gel she had smoothed on her skin had drawn the heat from the burns. Caspia stared at her palms. The blisters had dried. The skin was clear apart from faint red traces like speckles on the silver skin of river fish. She flexed her fingers.

She watched the shadows in the small room lengthen, hurled her shoe as a black rat pushed under the door. She missed and the rat sat as she tugged off her other shoe, then ran up the wall and out through the tiny window. She heard footsteps.

Azbarak stood in the doorway, a grey healer cloak over his arm, a bag in his hand. He put his finger to his lips and beckoned. Caspia put on her shoes and took the cloak he held out for her, slipping it round her shoulders. Azbarak pulled up the hood, hiding her hair. She followed him. He moved swiftly, as light and quiet as a cat. They met no one in the palace. No one held the pony that stood, head down in the square outside the gates. Cupping his hands so that Caspia could step into them, Azbarak tossed her up into the saddle and passed her the back-sack.

'Food. Gold. A knife. Clothes.' He wheezed as he bent to

release the leather thongs round the pony's fetlocks. 'And Elin's rings. Keep the hood up until you are clear of the city. Find Zartev, the old Wulf Kin, if he still lives. He will protect you.'

Caspia stared down at him. 'Why are you doing this?'

'For what was.' He smiled at her. 'I was there to announce your birth. I have watched you grow. I served your mother's mother and your mother.'

Caspia's eyes narrowed. 'And who do you serve now?'

'The city. As always.' He stepped away from the pony. 'Go now.'

Caspia gathered the reins. 'And my mother?'

'Will rest with Urteth at the Tower of Eagles.'

'She must have a queen's burial,' said Caspia.

Azbarak nodded. 'The Catcher has promised it.'

Caspia snatched at his thoughts. She found nothing beyond the things he'd told her.

'See that she keeps her word.'

She raised her clenched fist, touched it to her forehead and, drumming her heels against the pony's flanks, rode quickly away before he could see the brightness in her eyes.

Azbarak watched until the pony and its rider had vanished into the narrow tangle of streets that led to the city gates. He stooped to pick up the ties that he had dropped onto the ground and shuddered as he saw the black rat with a crooked tail nibbling the leather. It was a good thing that rats couldn't talk. Swiping Tiki aside, he hurried back into the palace.

He didn't see the rat scurry across the square and leap onto Var's outstretched palm.

CHAPTER THIRTY-FIVE

K odo smoothed the silk beneath his fingers as he found the threads of a new story.

'I thought I'd be a trader,' he said.

'You'll trade in memories and stories instead of furs and pots. And you can still go with Trader to new places,' Maia reminded him. She looked at the coat spread across Kodo's knees. 'Perhaps with a lizard boy to sing its stories the silk will cross water without fearing it.'

Kodo rummaged beneath the silk and pulled out a sleepy rat. He dropped it beside Nefrar's paws. 'I hope you weren't nibbling it,' he said, knowing full well that the cloth would have shrieked in protest if Tiki had been. He folded the coat and tucked it into the travel-stained bag.

Nefrar flexed his claws. The rat scampered towards Var who scooped him up as he approached. He placed the rat on his shoulder.

Maia sat up.

'Don't leave,' she said.

Kodo scrambled to his feet. 'I promised Huan I would ride with him,' he said. 'Are you coming?' he asked Var.

Var nodded, watching a bird high above the city beneath towering storm clouds.

'You're leaving,' she said.

'Yes.'

'To find the Kuma?' she guessed.

Var hesitated.

'And if I asked you to stay?'

Var was silent.

Maia nibbled her thumbnail. 'I wasn't going to ask,' she said. 'I know you want to go.'

Var squatted beside her. 'If you ask I must stay,' he said.

'Oh!'

Var took the white pebble from his tunic. Maia saw that the runes were little more than the twisting silver track of a snail. He placed the stone on her palm, closing her fingers over it. It was warm from his skin.

'The Kuma have many things to teach me,' he said. 'I had lost much when Azbarak found me wandering alone. I need to return. I need to listen to the sounds and silence of the desert. To find my . . . has-been.'

Maia remembered the endless hot land and how she had felt she belonged there. Had wondered if the rock paintings of the Sun Catcher showed the has-been, or what was yet to come.

'To be alone,' she said. She opened her hand and traced

the faint pattern of the runes. 'Hidden.'

Var looked at her bent head. Was she talking about him or the land? He thought that perhaps they were the same.

He touched the stone with his fingertip. 'If you need me,' he said, 'The Watcher's stone will find me.'

Their eyes met.

Maia attempted a smile. 'And if I follow the stone into the desert, what will I find? A white bird, with the wingspan of an eagle?'

Var's answering smile was like light at sun-wake. 'Perhaps.'

Maia watched Azbarak lead the city dwellers into the solar. They walked in wide-eyed silence, cast curious glances up at the painted roof with its gold moon and stars, touched the carved pillars decorated with swirling patterns of plants and animals. The banners on the walls shivered as people drifted along the wide avenue between the pillars and massed behind the vast hearth.

The solar was full of light. It shone on the stone throne where she sat as Queen. She smiled when someone dared to meet her eyes and was pleased that most had the courage to smile back even if their gaze did flicker to the spotted cat who stood between the stone chairs, his amber eyes reflecting the blaze of the many torches Azbarak had placed around the solar.

She wondered if Kodo, who sat beside her, felt as strange

as she did. She knew he hoped that Trader Bron's ship was in port. That he would be there in the crowd. She searched the faces looking for the sunburst beard and hair of the man whose ship had carried them back to the Cliff Village.

She thought she glimpsed the golden beard and wild hair of Bron standing with Yanna and Tareth and glanced at Kodo to see if he had seen him too. Kodo's hands were smoothing the silk. She knew if she listened hard she would hear the silk sighing like the sun-deeps as sea-rise surged between the huts in his Stilt Village.

She watched Var talking to Azbarak and the tall acrobat, Nimah. She saw the Keeper throw up his hands in exasperation. Var and the dark-haired girl remained at the edge of the firelight after he left them. They were silent, standing close, their hands not quite touching. Maia could tell that they were old friends, perhaps more.

She saw Var watch the girl depart, his face bleak. And then he was surrounded by leaping, tumbling children waving banners, jugglers, acrobats, girls beating hand drums. Azbarak's children dragged him as if he belonged to them still and took up their positions in front of the dais, following Nimah in her flame-coloured tunic as she smiled and cartwheeled and danced across the solar. They spun through the crowds until the hall was a mass of colour and movement, and rang with cries of delight and laughter.

Maia could hear Kodo beating out the rhythm with his fist on his knee and the high 'He! He!' call of the Hunters as if they were flying their eagles. The Sun Palace was full of life. Maia saw Zena who had woven the coat of many colours which she now wore. She was giggling with Huan who stood with Egon and a band of Eagle Hunters in their brilliant embroidered tunics. There was even a scatter of Warrior Women, their hair plaited with braids of many hues. She thought about the Watcher and Razek, the Storm Chaser, and wished they could see this too.

Maia laid her hand on Nefrar's head. How could she think she would be left alone in an empty stone palace when Var had vanished into the silences of the sands. She was the Sun Catcher. She had all the people in the Sun City to care for.

The silk sighed as Kodo got up from his chair.

She rose.

Kodo felt as if he was standing on the edge of the far-deeps. Instead of waves, there was a tide of people. Instead of the slap of water, a deep waiting silence. He stretched out his arms. He could hear the lizards singing and the strange crystal voices that must be songs from the stars. He felt the twist of a long-forgotten tale of tall flame-haired women striding through a desert. And songs from the snows on high mountains. He understood this was what he was meant to do.

He lowered his arms. The silk murmured.

'Story Singer,' it whispered. 'Sing.'

Kodo felt a flutter of panic. So many stories.

He looked at the slender, flame-haired Sun Catcher watching him. And knew the story he wanted to tell.

BRONZE AGE INFLUENCES

Sun Catcher is a magical reality story set in an imagined Bronze Age. It's a fascinating time. A time of change.

The Bronze Age happened at different times in many parts of the world so it's possible to 'borrow' ideas from many cultures: artifacts, ideas, customs, buildings. I've done this in *Sun Catcher*.

Thanks to archaeologists we know quite a lot about this period but wonderful new discoveries are being made all of the time. It's really exciting that the ingenuity and skills of Bronze Age people are continuing to intrigue and surprise us. I think that people who lived thousands of years ago were just like us, curious, innovative people who were engineers, artists, explorers, astrologers, herbalists, even scientists. They managed without computers and the internet and steam, electric or oil powered engines. But, like us they were busy shaping and changing their world. They told stories, exchanged ideas and passed their knowledge down through the generations.

Since our ancestors were very practical and intelligent and understood the world they lived in, I think that many of the imaginary things from *Sun Catcher* would be feasible in the Bronze Age and perhaps one day we'll even discover that this was so.

NAMES

I often found when I was writing the story that things I thought I had imagined and made up actually had some basis in reality. This was especially true when I was naming things, trying to make them sound as if they were from a distant past. Some historians think that there were no kings and powerful leaders in Bronze Age society, but I wanted a powerful warrior figure who could protect the land from Sea Raiders. I imagined the Marsh Lords and they needed a stronghold. I thought I would have to invent a neat word to describe it. I liked the word hold. I eventually decided that holdfast was a good name as Helmek the Marsh Lord holds tight or fast on to his land and his power. This seemed the perfect made-up name. But holdfast is not actually my invented term. After I'd written the story I discovered it is the name of the root that attaches seaweed to rocks. So I wasn't nearly as clever as I thought I had been. What is amazing is that the word holdfast fits so well because of course seaweed is important to Maia's adopted tribe.

TRADING

We know that Bronze Age people travelled great distances using both overland and sea routes and at the time my daughter was sailing round the world in a race on a yacht not much bigger than a Bronze Age boat. This gave me the idea for Kodo's dreams and adventures. He joins Bron, a sea-faring Bronze Age trader. Bron's imagined ship with its painted figurehead is probably more seaworthy and bigger than Bronze Age boats although they did have large ships and they did sail along extensive trading routes. So this is the true bit about Kodo's dream. However, this is not a history book and so Kodo . . .

'. . . *heard the creak of wood on wood. The voices rose and fell. Suddenly his world was full of the crash of oars, the chant of rowers, the cry of their Oar Master. Above him, a dragon with green eyes and gaping jaws emerged from the mist to swallow him... Kodo made out figures pulling at ropes, lowering the limp russet brown sail as the boat disappeared, leaving a spreading wake and a falling song.'*

Yes, they did sew the planks together to build boats. Yes, they did have oars, sweep oars for steering and sails. I don't know if they had painted figureheads or if they sang as they rowed or had an oar master to keep them rowing in unison. But why not? They did carry cargo and people. We know this because wrecks have been discovered and because many things, pottery, weapons and jewels have been found a long way from the place where they were made. Precious things were traded too. The blue beads Laya covets at the Gather would probably have come from Egypt or perhaps the beads were lapis lazuli a wonderful blue stone that would have been mined in Afghanistan.

People or tribes who lived in areas with rich mineral deposits became wealthy. So if you had access to copper, tin, gold, silver, salt, rare wood, ivory or lapis lazuli gem stones, people would want to trade with you and you could become rich and powerful in the Bronze Age. So in *Sun Catcher*, the Salt Holder is the richest man living near the cliff dwellers.

TIME

Time is something you have to think about in a story like *Sun Catcher* which doesn't happen in one day or in one place. There were no mechanical clocks in the Bronze Age. Well, none have been found. They would have measured time using what they could see; the sun, phases of the moon, maybe the shift of star constellations, tides, changes in plants and animal and bird migrations. Some civilizations did invent calendars. Seasons, solstices and equinoxes were important, special times for people in ancient societies. Meeting for festivals and trade at special places at certain times of the year certainly happened. So Maia goes to a Gather close by the holdfast and horse meadows and sees people from many different places.

To have a sun catching ceremony at solstice fits with

the importance of the sun and the seasons of the year for people dependent on farming. The successful planting and harvesting of crops could mean the difference between life and death. If there really was such a person as a Sun Catcher they would have been very important.

HOMES

Many people were still nomadic in the Bronze Age, which means that they moved from one place to another, so there are horse herders on Maia's journey, and nomadic shepherds, as well as settled communities. Around this time hunter gatherers were being replaced by settled families in areas where food was plentiful and where farmers had learned to grow grain. Houses were being built, and in some places villages, towns, and even cities, were growing.

If there were habitable caves I think there would still have been cave dwellings as well as bone burial caves. So for the Cliff Dwellers and Maia to live in a kind of cave village on the edge of an ocean seemed an interesting idea. Transitional places, places on the edge, and boundaries were important to people in the past. People often lived near water so the cliff village by the sea, a boundary between one world and another, seemed a good place for a settlement, especially as seaweed is a rich source of food and of course the cliff dwellers would have fished too.

GAMES AND SPORTS

Games and sport were part of Bronze Age life, and in *Sun Catcher*, Tareth knocks over his gaming board and pieces.

I always assumed that like us Bronze Age people would enjoy playing board games and that they would make their own gaming pieces. We know that the Egyptians played board games. I was fascinated to read a few days ago that 49 small stone gaming pieces, dice and three shell and stone tokens have been found in an archeological dig in Turkey. I wonder just how many of the goods on Bron's boat originally came from that area too . . .

CLOTHES

Bronze Age people liked adorning themselves, their clothes and their horses. Roaming tribes had gold ornaments on their horse bridles. Many of these were of plants and animals. The horses ridden by the warrior women have these.

'The icy wind churned through the standing horses, whipping their manes into a frenzy. Gold harness ornaments swung and glinted in the pale sunshine.'

Huan, the Eagle Hunter, would have decorated his horse's bridle too. Bronze Age jewelry was beautiful. Brooches, or stab pins, were used to close garments as well as to decorate them and to show how wealthy or important the person wearing them was. They are made from bone, gold, precious stones; Maia is given a silver stab pin.

People were often buried in their finest clothes with prized objects and jewelry, and so, in *Sun Catcher*, Maia's sister, Xania, has an elaborate burial.

TATTOOS

Bronze Age people would have known about tattooing. There were many reasons for having a tattoo, not just for making the skin of the wearer look beautiful. Often they had special meanings or purposes. Tattoos could have been magic symbols to help heal rheumatism or an injury or tribal markings or decorations and symbols to mark ceremonial rite of passage.

I wanted my characters to have tattoos too. The Lizard people have tattoos on their thumbs. This is how Kodo realizes that the powerful Marsh Lord must have been one of the Lizard People. Zena has a tattoo on her neck. Xania has a leaping cat tattooed on her wrist. Xania's tattoo has the same design as the special silver stab pin Maia has been given. A pin that belonged to her mother. This helps convince Maia that the stranger is her sister.

TOOLS, WEAPONS AND ARMOUR

Although bronze was a new technology, people in the Bronze Age still used old tool making skills too. I decided that the community of seaweed farmers would still be using flint for knives and tools. Bronze weapons would be high status and expensive so at first probably only important or rich people would have them.

Razek, as Weed Master, wants a metal knife. This is why he decides to keep the dead Wulf Kin's silver and bronze and eventually trades the stolen silver armband at the Gather with disastrous consequences.

Tareth comes from a different land and lived in the Sun Palace, so he would also have had valuable, state-of-the-art weapons. Luckily he did not lose everything when he was shipwrecked with Maia near the cliff village so he has metal as well as flint knives.

Tareth is the Warrior Weaver. As well as being trained in unarmed combat skills, Tareth also has a bow. So do the warrior women. They hang their silk wrist bracelets on their bows to give the bows special powers. Their bows are used for hunting but of course they are weapons too. I wanted Tareth's bow to be precious and special so it has a name, Blackwood. I think that special weapons would have been given names because their owners believed the weapons had magical powers. If I was a warrior and had a special weapon I think I would name it too.

Whenever I visit the British Museum I go and see the

wonderful galleries exhibiting gold and treasures troves and weapons from the Bronze Age and visit the Sutton Hoo treasures. The famous Sutton Hoo helmet is later than Bronze Age but Bronze Age warriors did have shields and helmets, swords and spears so it was easy to imagine the Marsh Lord with his helmet.

Maia's sun catching helmet with its silk eye pieces woven by Tareth to protect her eyes from the glare of the sun would have been much more elaborate and precious than these. I'm hoping one day that somewhere in a drowned or buried treasure trove a beautiful gold helmet will be discovered to remind me that *Sun Catcher* was influenced by the Bronze Age although I don't expect there to be any traces of the mysterious magical whispering silk. But who knows? Perhaps hidden in a dusty cabinet in a dark forgotten corner in a museum or folded in an ancient chest in an attic the moon-moth silk is singing.

Sheila Rance
West Sussex
August 2013

Acknowledgements

Writing this is always the easiest and yet the hardest part of a book. It means that an amazing adventure, the telling of a story, is over for a while so the task is tinged with sadness as well as pleasure. Maia has found a Story Singer and has to thank her friends and companions, so have I.

As always, first thanks go to Dave and my family, my bright stars. Dave kept the holdfast safe as I wandered off into the Hidden and my family have put up with my absentmindedness as I chased after a Sun Catcher and sometimes forgot them. I couldn't find the story without you all.

No book is a solo effort. Many hands make light work and make the dreams possible. John McLay, my agent, was there at the beginning and is now an honorary warrior, although he can be one of the Eagle Hunters if he prefers. I'm very lucky to have the safe hands of my wonderful editors at Orion, Fiona Kennedy and Felicity Johnston, ready to catch and improve the story. Behind the scenes, the support of Nina Douglas and the rest of the Orion Children's Book team has once again been amazing and is much appreciated. The party was fun too. The new illustrations by Geoff Taylor surprised and delighted me. I love seeing the characters come to life in his pen and ink drawing. Thank you.

Special thanks to Theo. Now you know what happens next.

And of course, high fives and huge thanks for the input and good will of all the friends and readers who eagerly travelled with me into Khandar to discover the next adventure. You have been the best of companions.

Sheila Rance
One Sunday afternoon, by a winter fire,
in that timeless place between one adventure and the next
West Sussex
December 2014